UNDER NEW MANAGEMENT

One by one the women wound their way through the barroom, draped themselves over the laps of customers, leaned provocatively against the bar. A girl in powder blue leaned over, laughing while a man stuffed money down her cleavage with one hand and patted her behind with the other. Another girl had already snared a victim, and was leading him toward us.

I had been sheltered, to be sure, but not so sheltered that I believed actresses—even common dancers—would do things like this!

I had been a complete dolt, and reality overtook me like a douse of ice water.

"We're all yours, honey," announced Belle, her smile broad.

As the girl and her grinning client climbed past us, I stammered, "It's a . . . it's a . . . it's a . . . it's a . . ."

"Best damn whorehouse in the whole damn country," Belle said proudly, and dragged me back up the stairs.

THE
LEGENDARY
KID DONOVAN

E. K. Recknor

A SIGNET BOOK

SIGNET
Published by New American Library, a division of
Penguin Group (USA) Inc., 375 Hudson Street,
New York, New York 10014, USA
Penguin Group (Canada), 90 Eglinton Avenue East, Suite 700, Toronto,
Ontario M4P 2Y3, Canada (a division of Pearson Penguin Canada Inc.)
Penguin Books Ltd., 80 Strand, London WC2R 0RL, England
Penguin Ireland, 25 St. Stephen's Green, Dublin 2,
Ireland (a division of Penguin Books Ltd.)
Penguin Group (Australia), 250 Camberwell Road, Camberwell, Victoria 3124,
Australia (a division of Pearson Australia Group Pty. Ltd.)
Penguin Books India Pvt. Ltd., 11 Community Centre, Panchsheel Park,
New Delhi - 110 017, India
Penguin Group (NZ), cnr Airborne and Rosedale Roads, Albany,
Auckland 1310, New Zealand (a division of Pearson New Zealand Ltd.)
Penguin Books (South Africa) (Pty.) Ltd., 24 Sturdee Avenue,
Rosebank, Johannesburg 2196, South Africa

Penguin Books Ltd., Registered Offices:
80 Strand, London WC2R 0RL, England

First published by Signet, an imprint of New American Library,
a division of Penguin Group (USA) Inc.

First Printing, September 2005
10 9 8 7 6 5 4 3 2 1

December 14, 1938
Phoenix, Arizona

Mr. Horace Smith III
Smith, Smith, Riley & Proctor
New York City, New York

My dear Trey,

I wrote these pages years ago, right after your father was killed in the Great War. I felt guilty for never having told him the truth. Still do. So I penned this confession, intending to leave it to you when I passed. However, your imminent inauguration as senator from my home, the great state of New York—and all the yellow journalism that will inevitably follow—forces my hand, and I herewith mail it to you.

Of course, you've heard of Kid Donovan. When your father and uncle were youngsters, they used to play at him, taking turns being the Kid or Cole Jeffries at that last shootout in Diablo. Years later, you played the same game with your friends—and accidentally set the garage afire, as I remember. I imagine half the children in the country played in the same way.

Your grandmother and I used to tell you the same thing we'd told your father—that there had never been a Kid Donovan, that he was nothing but a dusty old legend.

That wasn't exactly true.

Kid Donovan existed, all right, but only for a scant five months. It was just enough time to bring down a ring of scrofulous stock swindlers and avoid certain disaster on Wall Street; just enough time to kill countless men and burn down a town, and to turn part of the Arizona Territory—and half of New York City, I daresay—on their collective ears.

I should know, because I was Kid Donovan. I admit to the name—though not half the charges—and I also admit to a little whoremongering. After all, what else can a sixteen-year-old boy do when his only living relative—make that his last relative on this earth to die—bequeaths him the finest whorehouse in Pinal County, Arizona?

Shocked, are you? I know what you're thinking, but I assure you, your old grandfather is still in his right mind.

I have written the whole of it, from Mother and Father to Cole and Belle, to Jingles and Lop Ear, and to that larcenous backstabber Aloysius Dean, who hired none other than the infamous shootist John Henry Strider to come after me. That bloody incident marked the birth of Kid Donovan, and set me off on a course from which I barely escaped alive.

But I'm getting ahead of myself. Have no fear, Trey. Here in these pages I have laid it all bare with nothing held back for the sake of either modesty or shame.

Do with it what you will, my boy. Use as needed, as the doctors say.

Fondly,
Grandfather

1

I was sixteen years old on the very day I stepped off the train in Flagstaff, Arizona—fresh from the cosseted upper-middle class of New York City—but I hadn't much cause for celebration.

Quite the opposite, in fact. Just six weeks earlier, both my parents had been the victims of a freakish accident. They'd been on holiday in the south of France, taking in the sights from the comfort of a hired four-in-hand, when their coach went off a cliff. Their coachman leapt clear and the horses escaped injury, the shaft having given way, but Mother and Father were there one minute and sloshing against Mediterranean rocks the next.

I comforted myself that Mother had always loved the sea, and that she had finally gotten Father to take a dip, albeit permanently.

I don't mean to sound callous. I suppose I hadn't seen much of them, having been away at school most of the years since I was quite small, and so it wasn't as if I had been constantly seeking—or receiving—their comfort and nurture. I admit that I was closer to my chemistry instructor and my riding master—and I daresay most of the groundsmen—than I was to my father. And I held Mrs. Slaughter, the housekeeper at Billings Hall, dearer than I did my own mother.

I knew her so much better, you see.

Home was a place I visited every two or three years, when my parents weren't in Europe. Or when my mother wasn't plagued by one of her frequent—and long-lingering—headaches. Sometimes they would last, very conveniently, for the entire summer vacation and recur again at Christmas break. At these times I was shunted off to the homes of school friends or, worse, sent off on "educational trips" with paid companions. So far as I was concerned, home was little more than the place the money came from.

It's probably a sin to say such things, but it's the truth.

At any rate, it was a very disheartened youth who stepped down to the Flagstaff platform that tenth day of May in the year 1882. There I stood, in my best charcoal suit of clothes—from which my knobby wrists and bony ankles were swiftly emerging—and there was no Uncle Hector in sight, not a blessed soul to meet me.

Sullen, I sat on a bench, my trunks carelessly stacked at my side, and sulked. I had quickly lost any fascination I'd once held for trains after the third day out. A fair-sized cinder in the eye will do that for a person. But I waited obediently on the platform with the trains coming and going, disgorging the flotsam and jetsam of America, it seemed to me, while reeking of hot metal and burned oil and sending out huge jets of steam. These jets turned the blowing dust from the streets into a slick slime and silt that settled into every pore, and shortly turned my dark gray suit to the color of ashes.

And all the time that I sat there, I was thinking that I didn't deserve to be bundled off to a town called Tonto's Wickiup. I didn't deserve to have to live above a place called Hanratty's. I had no clue what Hanratty's might be, mind you, just that it was Uncle Hector's place of business, and that he lived upstairs.

I deserved to have my life back, I thought as I sat there with the steam jetting and the metal complaining, and disreputable fellows—ax murderers one and all, no doubt—clambering off and on the trains.

I deserved to finish prep school, and set out for the ivied halls of Harvard when the time came. I deserved to be sculling the streams of New England and playing tennis and riding to the hounds, and investigating the mysteries of Miss Olivia MacKember's Academy for Young Ladies of Good Breeding, across the Hudson.

I considered everything that had happened to me to be a slap in my face by God, Himself, who had apparently—and for no particular reason—taken a sudden and distinct dislike to me.

At any rate, after two hours of feeling good and sorry for myself—something I'd honed to an art those past two months—and of pacing and sitting and checking my watch and pacing some more, Uncle Hector still had not come.

This was the final insult to my many injuries. Uncle Hector was my mother's only brother and my only living relative, and it was to his home in Tonto's Wickiup that Misters Dean and Cummings, father's attorneys, had packed me off.

I can't say that I gave them a great deal of argument. I can't say that I really took in a quarter of what they said in those dark, stuffy legal offices, amid the smells of old leather and ink and lemon oil.

I was only a boy, after all. A very cloistered boy, although I didn't see it at the time.

At any rate, the part that did sink in was that Father had been deep in debt, and there was nothing for me, nothing. Goodbye to Tattinger Prep, the only true home I'd known, for there was no more tuition money now that I had completed the term. No more Manhattan brownstone to visit on those selected holidays when I was invited. No more servants, no more thundering rides after the hounds, no more riding boots ordered direct from London. Hardly more than the clothes on my back.

I had studied a map, of course, to pass the time on the train. I had worn it to tatters, actually. And the only conveyance between Tonto's Wickiup and Flagstaff—between Flagstaff and practically anything south, west, or north of it—appeared to be the Butterfield stage route. If Uncle Hector didn't come tonight—and I had already decided that he wasn't coming, the thoughtless wretch—I determined to set out and meet him on his way.

Of course, this entailed finding a hotel for the night, and I reluctantly checked my purse. Mr. Dean had taken pity on me before I left New York, and pressed fifty dollars into my hand. It was a sum that I would have once spent on clothes or trinkets without a second thought. It was the only money I possessed, and I now had only thirty-two dollars and twenty cents remaining.

I left my trunks under what I hoped was the watchful eye of the station master, jotted down the directions he gave me, and made my way toward the hotel.

The town, if you could call it that, was appalling. I supposed I should have paid more attention to Clive's battered dime novels. Clive Barrow was my roommate back at Tattinger's, and he probably had hundreds of the things, mostly centering on the West and concerning desperadoes and shootists and cattle rustlers and wild Indians and the like. I had always thought they were silly, childish. But now, as I nervously walked the streets of Flagstaff, certain there were gunmen or bandits in every shadowed alley, I wished I'd read them like primers.

Luckily, the hotel wasn't far, but I almost didn't go inside. No stately marble pillars here, no uniformed doorman, no glass and brass and burnished wood. Just a sign that said COBB'S—CLEAN BEDS and a tiny dingy lobby with one weak lantern to light it.

The front desk was little more than a plank set on two barrels, with a few mismatched keys hanging from nails on the wall in back of it. Once I had cleared my throat a few times and the man behind the desk put his newspaper aside, he eyed me curiously.

"From back east, ain't you?" he asked by way of a greeting, and turned the register toward me.

I didn't deem this worthy of an answer, and elaborately wrote my name, as was my affectation of the moment, with many curlicues, and underlined it with a flourish. I returned the pen to its inkwell, flipped the register back toward him, and asked, in my most officious voice, "Where would the Butterfield office be, my good man?"

He didn't answer right away. He was too busy squinting at what I had written. "Horace Tate Pemberton Smith," he said at last, twisting his head back and forth and making the most of every syllable. He looked up. "By jingo, squirt! You sure they's only one a' you?"

I ignored the question, although I may have arched a brow. I did a good deal of eyebrow arching back then. "The Butterfield office, sir?" I repeated.

He leaned a hand on the desk and regarded me with a smirk in his eyes, as if he were privy to some secret joke. He said, "Well now there, Horace, the Butterfield's closed up for the night. Be open at seven on the dot, unless Jess's wife's been drinkin' again and don't wake him up. Where 'bouts you headed?"

The clerk provided me a wobbly handcart, with which I collected my belongings and brought them back to the hotel. After a furtive fried egg dinner at a hole in the wall called Aunt Mary's Eats, I fairly raced upstairs to my room and locked the door behind me. I also barricaded it with the room's sole chair. Shaking, I hunched across the narrow room on the bed, my back pressed to the wall.

If Tonto's Wickiup was anything like Flagstaff, where I'd just seen one man shoot another in the kneecap over a side order of fried onions, it was a place in which I had no business.

Somehow, I managed to sleep—still sitting up and in all my clothes—and woke with the dawn. After I ferried my things to the still-closed Butterfield office, I made yet another trip to the train depot to inquire about Uncle Hector. He still hadn't shown his face, and I resigned myself to making the rest of the journey alone.

This saddened me tremendously. I'd come all the way from New York by myself, of course, but I was counting on Uncle Hector's company—even if should turn out to be bad company—for the remainder of the trip. When you are just one day past sixteen, you can only stand so much of being alone.

True, I had been alone for most of my life. Surrounded by the other boys at school, certainly, and there were always servants at hand. But, all in all, I'd been alone, even in the crowd at Tattinger's. I suppose that somewhere deep inside, I was wishing that Uncle Hector would turn out to be a true uncle, not only in blood, but in heart. A secret part of me, you see, still lived in hope.

At any rate, when the 9:30 stagecoach arrived at seventeen past ten—"Right on time," quipped Jess, the lanky station master, with a glance at his pocket watch—I loaded my trunks with the help of one Mr. Muskrat Hutchins, the driver, then clambered aboard.

"Christ a'mighty, kid!" Muskrat Hutchins snarled through the open coach door. His grizzled and untrimmed mustache completely hid his mouth. "What the H-E-double-L you got in them trunks, anyways?"

"Everything," I said.

It was the truth.

The trip was long, and I was alone for the better part of it. We couldn't make very fast time in the mountains, and spent the next three nights at ramshackle stage stops. The food at each was worse than the last.

There was still no sight of—or word from—Uncle

Hector, although I inquired at each stop. The only thing working in my favor was that while we changed teams frequently, we changed coaches but once, and so I didn't have to help unload and reload my trunks over and over. Trust me, a trunk that weighs only forty or fifty pounds on the flat seems to weigh a hundred more when you are called on to hoist it overhead.

Once we left the mountains behind, it was comparatively easy going, if you could ignore the dire condition of the roads. I had company for small spurts of time. There was a fat, silent woman who said she lived near a town called Milcher and got off in the middle of nowhere, where her husband, I guessed, was waiting with a buckboard.

A drummer joined me on the leg of the trip from Peach Tree to Hanged Dog. At least he was talkative, but since he was fairly well oiled when he got on—and more so by the time he got off, due to frequent sips from a pocket flask—none of it made much sense.

And all the while, the view became more and more depressing. We were making fast progress over the vast plains, now. Sometimes they seemed to go on forever, flat to a horizon edged with distant, jagged mountains, with nothing between to break the monotony but cactus. Other times, a small chain of arid hills or a stand of rock—red or yellow or white or tan or all four, like a layer cake—would thrust from the plain. Some stood singly, like a dog's canine tooth, and some were clusters and spires and hummocks of rock the size of small villages.

Not a scrap of it, however, looked habitable.

As the landscape grew drier and hotter and more alien, I found myself yearning for the sweet-smelling pines of Flagstaff. Funny, but I hadn't considered them sweet, hadn't considered them at all, really, until just then.

I wouldn't have minded so much getting shot over fried onions, I thought. At least it was cooler up north, and the dust filtered down softly instead of blasting you in the face.

It's all a matter of degrees, isn't it? The things a person can stand, I mean, and still be alive.

And then yet another tatty little town came into sight. It was built right on the open plain, with no hills, no towering rocks, and hardly a tree to shelter it. Its mud-brick-and-plank buildings looked as if they'd just been dropped there by the hand of God, and some had shattered on impact.

"Welcome to Shit Hole," muttered the man across from me, who had boarded the stage three stops back and had suffered through the drunken salesman with me. It was the first thing that he'd said, although it was more of a mumble, and he said it more out the window than to me, personally.

He was a rough-looking fellow—about thirty, I supposed—with sandy hair, a stubbly, unshaven jaw, a wide mustache, and a gun strapped to each hip.

His guns looked to be in fine repair, even if he didn't. At least, they were shiny enough, and had fancy pearl grips with eagles carved into them.

It was all I could do not to ask to see one of them. Judging by his manner, though, I think I was wise not to.

We had entered the town by then. A handful of squealing hogs parted as we slowed, then stopped, in front of the Butterfield office.

My companion stepped down from the stage almost before it had stopped, and directly into the arms of a young woman. I mean that just the way it sounds. She squealed, "Cole!" and gripped him in an embrace the moment his spurs clanked on the boardwalk.

He did nothing to stop her, and I was transfixed, watching them, only jumping a little when Muskrat Hutchins tossed the man's saddle down after him. After all, my parents were not ones for public displays of affection, and the meetings and partings I'd observed on train platforms across the country were far less . . . carnal. I couldn't think of another word to describe this one.

Just then, Mr. Muskrat Hutchins broke into my thoughts. Actually, he nearly broke my neck, it snapped around so fast.

"Get out here and help me with these trunks a' yourn, Horace," he shouted, roughly a foot from my ear. He was hanging upside down from the top of the coach at the time.

We were on a first name basis by now—well, he was, anyway—and I had learned he was hard of hearing, the result of having a rifle discharged directly beside his ear during the Battle of Bull Run.

He had also imparted various desert survival tidbits to me, such as to never let your testicles dangle down the hole of an outhouse. This, he told me, was because of the black widows that liked to web there.

"One gets her fangs into you," he'd said with a scratch at his neck, "and your balls'll get swole up like musk melons. She'll put you in bed for a week if'n she don't kill you."

While this was certainly valuable information, I would rather that he hadn't shouted it in front of the Peach Tree station master's wife.

"You hear me, boy?" he shouted, still upside down. "This here's Tonto's Wickiup."

"Are you sure?" I yelled back, certain it was someplace with the unfortunate name of Shit Hole, but he only gave me an annoyed look.

As I struggled to get my land legs, Muskrat Hutchins pushed down trunk after trunk to me. The first one, I caught, and while I was still staggering under its weight, he tossed the other two to the ground. I heard something break. Muskrat Hutchins didn't, though. He just went on about his business.

Dejectedly, I shoved my luggage together and slumped on the nearest trunk, wondering whether it was the glass in a picture frame that had broken—

and if so, which one—and watching for anyone who looked like he might be my uncle.

By the time they'd changed the team, Muskrat Hutchins had waved goodbye, and the coach had left me in its dust—a trick accomplished in less than ten minutes—I was alone on the boardwalk. But across the way and down a little, through the space newly vacated by the stagecoach, I spied a large sign. HANRATTY'S, it proclaimed in large, elaborate letters.

To be honest, I nearly wept from the abject relief of it.

However, I did the manly thing. I swallowed the lump in my throat, stood up, gave my suit coat a tug, and dusted myself off the best I could. I grabbed hold of the first of my trunks and proceeded to drag it up the dusty street, past more squabbling hogs, toward Hanratty's.

2

Hanratty's was, of all things, a saloon.

I stood there, just inside the batwing doors, with my mouth hanging open. My uncle—my own mother's brother, for God's sake—owned a saloon?

I had ignored the CLOSED sign on my way in and the room was void of customers, but it was enormous. Perhaps a dozen large tables and as many smaller ones, their tops ringed with upturned chairs, sat round the floor. Above, chandeliers constructed from wagon wheels depended on ropes from the high ceiling, and in between the chandeliers, there hung several large five-bladed fans.

Lining the wall on my right were banks of glowing windows, edged with stained glass dragonflies and pond lilies that streamed fingers of purple and red and green light across the plank floor. Also to my right was a long, narrow staircase that led up to a railed balcony, perhaps eleven or twelve feet above me. It wrapped the flanks and back of the second floor, and multiple doors opened off it.

A sleek bar of polished cherry, complete with a brass foot rail and findings, ran nearly thirty feet along the wall to my left. The back bar was elaborate, and punctuated every few feet by paintings of naked women. There were long shelves for liquor bottles and glasses in between, and a huge mirror, flanked by cut crystal lamps, at the center.

At the rear of the room was a stage, draped by a red velvet curtain. I began to see a glimmer of hope. Not only did Uncle Hector have a prosperous and well-kept establishment, but he was in show business!

My parents wouldn't approve, but then, they weren't here, were they? And Uncle Hector had marvelous taste in paintings. My eye kept traveling back to one of a buxom blonde, invitingly stretched out on an electric blue sofa.

Oh, she was grand, just grand! You could see her nipples—both of them—and so far nobody had smacked me on the back of the head for looking at her, as had Mr. Haskell when he found us passing around Bobby Trask's French postcards in European History.

"Can I help you, kid?" said a sour voice, and my hand automatically flew to cover the back of my neck.

There was no danger, though—at least, none that was imminent. The man who had spoken stood behind me, wiping his large, chapped hands on a bar towel. He was tall, muscular, and clean-shaven, with a square, dour face. Dark hair fringed a wide bald spot.

"Y-yes," I stammered as I turned toward him, "you may indeed be of assistance."

"I asked what you wanted," he repeated.

"I should like to see Mr. Hector Pemberton, if you please," I said, and belatedly remembered to stand up straight and be a Smith, by God.

"Too late" was all the man said.

My heart sank. Uncle Hector had gone to meet the train after all, and was probably scouring Flagstaff for me at this minute. Probably cursing me, too.

It was not the most propitious start.

"When did he leave for Flagstaff?" I asked, rapidly calculating the time it would take him to get back in every possible instance. Mathematics was among my stronger suits. I hoped this man would see reason and allow me to stay at Hanratty's until Uncle Hector's return. I wanted to peruse that painting at my leisure.

The bartender tucked his chin and gave me quite a look. "Flagstaff? Why the hell would Mr. P. go up to Flag?"

Obviously, this man knew nothing. I needed to talk to his superior, and was about to tell him so when a flutey voice called out, "Willie? Hey, Willie, whatcha got down there?"

I looked up to see a woman leaning over the balcony rail. Wild red hair spun over her bare shoulders and framed a heart-shaped face. She had nothing on but a flimsy white chemise and short silk knickers of some sort, with a gauzy pink feather-trimmed robe tossed recklessly over them. The robe was open, and as she leaned casually on the railing, arms splayed, I could see deep into the shadows of her cleavage.

Now I had never seen a female in such an advanced state of undress—not a living, breathing one, at any rate—and it stopped me cold. Or hot, more likely. The sweat that had been seeping relentlessly from my pores since midmorning began to pour from me in rivers, gluing my clothing to my body, and all I could do was stare at her and gulp damply.

"That's what I'm tryin' to find out, Belle," the barkeep shouted back at her. Frowning, he turned back to me. "Your mama know you're in here?"

The thought of Mother—socially fastidious, always tastefully attired, and doubtless heartily disapproving of this situation, even though she was dead and therefore past doing anything about it—was the thing that at last allowed me to tear my gaze from the woman on the balcony.

The barkeep was snapping his fingers beside my ear by this time. "Hey! Over here!"

I took a deep breath. "My name is Horace Tate Pemberton Smith, sir, and Hector Pemberton is my uncle. I should like to wait for him here, if you don't mind," I said, and added, a tad pompously, "Even if you do."

Willie the bartender pulled back a little and tucked his chin. "Well, I'll be dogged," he said. "Believe you do look a little like him round the eyes. Your mama that gallivantin' sister of his? You Helen's kid?"

From up on the balcony, I heard the fair Belle shout, "Hey, Dixie! Hey, Pony Girl! It's Mr. P's nephew!" and looked up again in time to see door after door open, and tousled female heads pop out all down the row.

It was a veritable cornucopia of feminine pulchritude, and I marveled that Uncle Hector could fit so many actresses on Hanratty's small stage. Perhaps it was deeper than it looked. Perhaps they all danced in a close row with their arms linked, while they kicked their legs high and squealed.

I had heard of such dances coming newly from Paris, but needless to say, I hadn't seen them. Quite suddenly, I was looking forward to the prospect of sitting front row, center.

An anticipatory leer barely had time to take hold of my face when, over the hum of excited female conversation, Willie called, "Back inside, you hens, and paint your faces. Fifteen minutes till we open."

Like so many turtles pulling into their shells, the heads disappeared and the doors closed, although Belle remained where she stood. "He all right, Willie?" she called. "You all right, boy?"

It was nice of her to ask, but I didn't see why I shouldn't be absolutely champion. The worst of it—the wrench from Tattinger's, the disbursal of my parents' property, and my grisly trip west—was over. Now there was only Uncle Hector to wait for.

The thing had turned a distinct corner, I thought. Considering what I'd seen so far at Hanratty's, I'd fallen into the proverbial cream. Uncle Hector could teach me the business, and what a bold and exciting business it was! The West would not always be so wild, I reasoned, and the country was growing smaller every day, what with the railroads. Twenty or thirty years from now, I could see myself husbanding a vast chain of fine drinking establishments— no, hotels!—across the country.

I determined to write a letter to Clive Barrow the first chance I got. While he would be back at Tattinger's next fall, mooning over his Western dime novels, I would be living smack in the middle of his favorite setting, surrounded by high-kicking actresses, and well on my way to becoming a captain of industry.

Of sorts.

Father had made sounds about wanting me to go into business, hadn't he? I didn't recall his ever saying what kind.

"I am splendid, madam, and thank you for asking," I called up to her, and gave a tip of my hat. I believe I smiled. I may have even winked. "I should like a room, though, where I can await my uncle's return."

She didn't answer me. Instead, she looked down at Willie and, her tone reproachful, hissed, "Didn't you mail that damn letter?"

He slapped a hand over his heart and solemnly said, "First thing, Belle. Pinkie-finger swear."

"What letter?" I asked.

Apparently it had nothing to do with me, for Belle ignored my inquiry. She stood erect and smoothed her hair, for what little good it did on those wild russet gypsy curls. She pulled her flimsy negligee close about her, an action for which I was heartily sorry, and then pointed past me, to my dusty trunk. "That thing all you brung with you?"

"There are two more trunks and a valise at the Butterfield office," I allowed.

She said, "Willie?"

Grumbling, "Yeah, yeah," he tossed his bar towel to a table and exited the saloon, presumably to fetch my remaining luggage.

Belle fairly floated down the stairs, a vision in pink, dripping tiny feathers as she neared. As she stepped to the floor I doffed my hat and gave a slight bow. "Madam," I said.

"If you say so," she replied.

Now that she was closer, I saw that she was older than I by at least ten years, although still quite beautiful. And I also realized that she looked vaguely familiar. Just as this realization struck me, a door off the upstairs balcony—Belle's door—banged open, and a man wearing nothing but his long johns and his pistols marched out, waving an empty whiskey decanter.

"Goddamn it, Belle!" he roared. "How long's it take to fetch a bottle?"

I recognized him at once. It was Cole, my rough and silent companion from the stagecoach, and Belle was the woman who had so eagerly greeted him on the boardwalk. I believe I flushed, for my face and neck felt suddenly twenty degrees hotter.

"Gonna be a minute, sugar," she called to him. "Got something to take care of." She jabbed a thumb in my direction.

Cole snorted and dangled the decanter over the railing.

"Don't you dare," she said firmly. "That's German crystal."

And without a second look at him, she took my arm and shepherded me back through the empty barroom, back through a curtained doorway at the side of the stage, and into a little hall. She opened the door to a room that bore a brass plate announcing OFFICE, and just as she ushered me through it, we both heard the distant crash of shattering crystal.

"I ain't cleanin' that up, you sonofabitch," she shouted up the hall before she pointed me toward a leather chair. With a tiny flurry of feathers, she perched on the edge of the desk, crossed one arm over her bosom, and heaved a sigh.

Carefully covering her knees, where my vision was riveted at the moment, she said, "Gotta tell you something kinda rough, kid. You want a slug first?"

* * *

About ten minutes later, I took her up on that drink.

I do not recall the exact words she used to tell me about Uncle Hector. I only remember that I kept repeating, "Dead, everybody's dead!" over and over. I also remember that I must have wept a little, because she offered me a pressed linen handkerchief from the desk drawer.

The gist of it was that eleven days previous, while I was readying to leave New York, Uncle Hector had visited one of his mining concerns. He was alone for some reason, and had gone better than two hundred feet below the surface when the shaft collapsed.

And that, as Belle put it, was all she wrote. I hadn't known Uncle Hector was involved in mining, but by this juncture I was surprised by nothing.

Apparently, they were still trying to dig deep enough to retrieve the body.

Belle poured me two fingers of bourbon from Uncle Hector's private reserve, and at her urging, I downed it all at once.

I do not recommend this procedure.

While I sputtered and coughed, my eyes still tearing from the liquor, she aided me from the office, across the main floor of the saloon and past a preoccupied Willie—who was sweeping up what I assumed to be the last of the crystal decanter and who mumbled, "McGinty's goddamn hogs are loose on the street again"—and up that long flight of stairs to the balcony.

By this time, I was once again capable of speech and asked her, "What's to become of me? Where will I go?"

While I'd like to believe otherwise, I imagine this came out as a sort of gravelly whine.

But Belle dragged me up the last few steps, patted me on the hand, and said, "Now don't you worry, sugar. Belle'll take care of you. And you're gonna stay right here."

I wouldn't take charity, couldn't. It wasn't in my nature. I was a Smith after all, and I had my standards. Gone, however, were my dreams of those actresses squealing and showing fleeting glimpses of their underdrawers. Gone were my hopes of learning the business under Uncle Hector's tutelage, and of having a place again, one I could at last call home.

Despite the whiskey burning my throat and belly, I took hold of the hand rail and forced myself erect.

"I . . . I thank you for your very great kindness, Miss Belle," I said, forcing the words out. "It is deeply appreciated. However, I have no wish to be a burden. I shall be on my way."

I turned myself around and started dejectedly down the stairs. I hadn't the slightest idea where I intended to go, only that I wished it to be someplace where no one knew me, where I could crawl into a hole and pull it closed over myself until I thought what to do.

But with a shake of her head that set all those fiery curls bobbing, Belle caught my arm. "This is your place now, honey," she said in a tone that was soft and convincing. All things about Belle were soft and convincing. "Ain't you figured that out yet? I reckon near everything Mr. P owned, he left to you, Lord love him. There's no need to be runnin' off."

In my addled state, this possibility had not occurred to me, and frankly, I was stunned. I simply stared at her, openmouthed.

Now, during this conversation, Hanratty's had officially opened for the day's business. I turned my head at the sound of footsteps and saw the batwing doors creaking open and closed on their hinges and the customers slowly wandering in, their boots and spurs making clunks and clangs on the scarred planks. Willie was behind the bar, already pouring whiskey and drawing beer.

"This . . . all this belongs to *me*?" I asked, afraid to believe that my good fortune, so suddenly snatched away, had returned tenfold.

"This, and the Lucky Seven and the Aztec Princess," she said, smiling wide. "Oh, and I reckon half ownership in the Two Bit, down to Tombstone."

"And those would be . . . ?"

"Mines, sugar, mines. Two silver, one copper. 'Course, they ain't much. They was mostly a hobby with him. Mr. P didn't exactly have a nose for bright metal—leastwise bright metal that kept on comin'. But they're haulin' a fair amount of copper outta the

Lucky Seven. Or they were, till it caved on poor Mr. P," she added, and placed a hand over her heart.

I was about to halfheartedly quip that perhaps the Lucky Seven had been misnamed, when someone brushed past me. And giggled.

Two steps down, the girl turned and looked up from under a mass of blond curls, and said, "Hiya, sweet pants." She winked a heavily painted eye.

"Get a move on, Pony Girl," said Belle.

I was shocked! The creature had on little more than her underthings, and more and more similarly attired women were following after her, parade-like, to the whistles and hoots of the men downstairs.

One by one they shouldered past us and down to the main floor. They wound their way through the barroom, draped themselves over the laps of customers, leaned provocatively against the bar. One of them called for a whiskey, then plopped down at the piano, spraddle-legged, and began to play Chopin's "Minute Waltz." It crossed my mind that at her present tempo, the piece would take a good three or four minutes.

A girl in powder blue leaned over, laughing while a man stuffed money down her cleavage with one hand and patted her behind with the other. Another girl had already snared a victim, and was leading him up toward us.

I had been sheltered, to be sure, but not so sheltered that I believed actresses—even common dancers—would do things like this!

I had been a complete dolt, and reality overtook me like a douse of ice water.

"We're all yours, honey," announced Belle, her smile broad.

As the girl and her grinning client climbed past us, I stammered, "It's a . . . it's a . . . it's a . . . it's a . . ."

"Best damn whorehouse in the whole damn county," Belle said proudly, and dragged me back up the stairs.

The rooms to which Belle showed me were in a corner of the building, just down from her door. There was a good-sized main room, in which Willie had deposited my trunks, with a small bedroom opening off it at far left to make an L-shaped apartment.

"Mr. P had it done up special," Belle confided as she threw wide the dark blue curtains and opened the windows. "Used to be, it was four rooms for the girls. See?" she said, pointing to a faint vertical imperfection that buckled the cobalt wallpaper. "They busted down a wall here, and another one over there. Only the best for Mr. P."

After she commented that I looked a bit green and determined that I hadn't eaten since breakfast, Belle promised to send somebody up with food, then left, confiding, "That Cole's gonna be madder'n a wet cat!"

Which left me alone to stare at Uncle Hector's wallpaper. I tossed my hat to the horsehair sofa, stripped off my suit coat and vest, unbuttoned my collar, and fell into a leather wingback chair. I was sweated through, and the leather felt cool and comforting.

Poor Uncle Hector had gone to join Mother and Father, but unlike Father, he hadn't lost all his money on Wall Street. He'd left me a going concern and three mines. Well, one mine and two others that were little more than holes in the ground.

I wondered what might constitute a fair amount of copper. It sounded like Uncle Hector had a crew working the Lucky Seven, and one didn't hire a crew of men unless the mine was producing sufficient ore.

Or did one? More to the point, did Uncle Hector? It had sounded as if these mines of his were mere playthings, and only one was divulging anything of value. It might be better to divest myself of them as soon as possible, I reasoned, and hang on to the Lucky Seven until I could determine if its output was worth the payroll. After all, I thought with a sniff, penny wise, pound foolish.

There is nothing so haughty as a sixteen-year-old tycoon.

Someone rapped at the door. I opened it, fully expecting to see Willie. Instead, I found a sour-faced, middle-aged woman—this one fully clad, thank God, down to her stained apron and stout shoes—bearing a covered tray.

She shoved it at me and growled, "Ain't much."

And with that, she clumped down the stairs while I stood looking after her, openmouthed. The hoots and laughter from below soon snapped me back to reality, however, and I closed the door between us.

Her "ain't much" turned out to be a thick roast beef sandwich on fresh sourdough bread, still warm from the oven. This was accompanied by a small plate of sweet pickles and a large slice of apple pie smothered in cheese, along with a rather dusty bottle of sarsaparilla. I ate it up, every scrap and crumb, and carried the last of the soda pop back to the bedroom with me.

Whether it was the heavy meal, the abrupt intake of bourbon, or the revelation that I had been thrust into the role of teenage whoremaster—or perhaps all three—I was suddenly exhausted. I wanted nothing more than to lie down.

Like the outer room, the bedroom smelled faintly of good cigars and witch hazel, but there the similarity ended. The first room had been spacious and airy, with good quality furnishings, better than I had thought to find so far from civilization. But Uncle Hector's sleeping quarters were another matter.

The room was stuffy and papered in emerald—the latter being nice, I supposed—and the bed was almost elegant, if you happened to be a Spanish ambassador.

It was dark and heavy and elaborately carved with scenes of the Spanish court, circa fifteen hundred, and so large that it took up most of the floor. Shoved hard against the flocked wallpaper at the head and

the far side, it left just enough room for a small chif-
forobe and a washstand at its foot, and a narrow
walkway at its side.

The room's sole window was almost entirely covered by the massive headboard, and I saw immediately that there was no hope of getting to it, let alone
getting it open.   The bed itself proved quite comfortable, though, if you could ease past the idea that you
were about to be carried off to the Inquisition. Or
that possibly the bed itself was a device of
Torquemada himself, and that at any moment spikes
would jut down from the canopy and slowly lower
to impale the sleeping victim.

I couldn't for the life of me imagine how they had
gotten it up the stairs, let alone shoehorned it into
that tiny room.

But it was there, all right, so I took off my shoes
and prepared for a nap. However, once I got settled
on Uncle Hector's mattress, I couldn't stop my mind
from whirling. I lay there, staring up into the dusty
underside of a green damask canopy, thinking about
Belle and that Cole person, and about Mr. Aloysius
Dean and the fifty dollars he'd kindly stuffed into
my hand back in New York.

I thought about poor Uncle Hector buried beneath
all that copper ore, and about that strange, out-of-
place woman who had brought my food. A vision of
Mother and Father, their bodies caught in the tide
and battered by rocks, entered my mind, and was

quickly replaced—thank God—by one of Clive Barrow's shaggy head, bent over the letter that I still had to write to him.

Clive and I had roomed together at Tattinger's for the past three years, and were known collectively as "Salt and Pepper." Clive was dark, almost swarthy, with sharp black eyes and an athletic build. I, on the other hand, was blue-eyed and so fair that when I returned from one of my "educational trips" at summer's end, my blond hair was nearly white from the sun. It wasn't until the last term that I had shot up to surpass Clive's height, if not his weight. When I left Tattinger's, the jovial cries of "Salt and Pepper" were being replaced with "Scarecrow and Squat."

Though he bore it with good humor, I daresay that Clive was not amused. I know I wasn't.

And so I determined to give Clive a good account of what had transpired so far, and was mentally composing my letter when I heard sounds on the other side of the wall.

Now I am not by nature an eavesdropper. At school, when I could have easily overheard Mr. Dillard dressing down Skinny Whipple for allegedly cheating on his trigonometry final, I walked right on down the hall. And did I listen, ear to the door, when Franklin Hower and Fats Bentley had that fistfight over Franklin's sister? I should say not! I only stayed for half of it, and Clive filled me in on the rest later.

However, on this occasion, I didn't believe I could lift an arm, much less get up and walk into the next room. Out of sheer inertia, I lay there and tried not to listen.

But, boys being boys, I soon pressed an ear to the wall. The speakers were Cole and Belle, her room being next to mine, and they were arguing.

"Why not?" demanded Belle. She sounded quite angry. "Why won't you tell him? It's his goddamn mine, ain't it?"

"Knock it off, Belle," Cole snapped. "Ain't had the time to digest it."

"What's there to think over? He's here, and it's his. Why not tell him?"

"Because."

"Don't you 'because' me, Cole Jeffries! 'Specially after what we just done."

Cole laughed. "And will again, Belle. Now put down that doo-bob."

She snorted. I could almost see her crossing her arms over her chest. "It ain't a 'doo-bob.' It's a glass horse. And I'm about ready to crown you with it, you sonofabitch, if you don't come clean with that kid. Besides, you busted the last of my German crystal. I brung that set all the way from El Paso!"

It was at this point that I belatedly determined it was me they were arguing about—well, me and the crystal—and I suddenly wished for a drinking glass to amplify the sound. I pressed harder against the wall.

"Belle, baby," Cole said, a bit softer, "I'll order you new stuff, a whole set. And it ain't safe to tell him yet. It's for his own good. I can't prove nothin', but I still got a feelin' that Heck didn't exactly die accidental.''

I gulped, for Heck had to be none other than Uncle Hector.

"But you can't prove nothin'," Belle insisted. "You said so yourself."

"I just got a feeling, okay?"

Belle made a hmphing sound.

"Trust me, baby," he said, so quietly that I barely heard it. "Just wait. From what you told me, he's had it pretty damn rough. Let him be a kid a while longer."

"Funny, you bein' so soft."

"Ain't soft. I just remember what it was like, that's all. Bein' a kid and havin' it yanked away."

There was a small sound, as if Belle had just put down whatever it was she was going to throw at him, and then she said, "You promise? About the crystal?"

"Promise," he said.

And then they lapsed into silence. Shortly thereafter, I lapsed into sleep.

3

When I woke, the raucous music and laughter vibrating the floor told me that Hanratty's was still in full swing.

I lit the lamps in my rooms, opened one trunk, and found fresh clothing. But none seemed right, somehow. I seemed to have grown at least a half inch since leaving New York City, and in more ways than one.

The last half day in Tonto's Wickiup, more than the last ten days in transit, had proven to me that I had been plunged into a vastly different world than I was used to inhabiting. My usual dark suits, no matter how immaculately tailored, had no more place here than a duck in a wolf's den. With a sigh, I laid the suit of clothes aside and opened Uncle Hector's wardrobe.

He'd had very good taste. I'll give him that. I was soon attired in a pair of tan striped britches, a light blue shirt, and a silk-fronted vest that were only a little too big for me. It was a welcome change to be able to move my arms.

I stood before the mirror and had a good look at myself. The clothes were more in keeping with my present situation, but the boy inside them seemed hopelessly out of place. No matter how I tried, I looked pasty-faced and startled, for all the world like a rabbit caught in a train lamp's glare.

Sleep had brought me back to reason, and despite my earlier—if brief—sense of confidence, I was totally out of my element. I could only hope for the kindness of Belle and her cohorts to see me through, to ease me into this strange new world.

And I intended to see if I couldn't find out why Cole was suspicious about my uncle's death— without letting on that I'd eavesdropped, of course.

I gave my vest a forceful tug, stood up to my full height—currently five feet and eleven and one half inches, with no end to it in sight—and stepped out to the balcony. Below, Belle caught my eye, and interrupted her conversation with one of the girls to lift a hand and beckon me down the stairs.

By the number of men crowding the bar rail and the tables, it was obvious that while the girls of Hanratty's were a draw, they were not the principal business of the place.

I passed a faro game with men crowded all around, and heard the rapid clicking of a roulette wheel's marble. All manner of men—brocade-vested dandies; gun-toting cowboys; weary shopkeepers and rough customers in fur hats; white and colored and Chinese and Mexican alike—played cards or threw the dice amid fan-churned clouds of yellow smoke.

Cole was nowhere to be seen. The girls were present, however, colorful dots floating on the crowd. A red speck atop the piano, an amber shimmer at the bar rail, a teal flutter in a cowboy's lap, and so on. They didn't overwhelm the place as they had seemed to earlier, but seemed more like a sprinkling of sugar candy, added for color.

Willie was still working the bar, but he had been joined by two more bartenders, and they were all busy pouring whiskey and beer and taking money. Despite my unease with nearly everything else, the money made me happy.

Once I'd made my way over to Belle, I half-expected her to instruct me to stand on a chair while she announced to one and all that I was the new proprietor. Perhaps all the men in the bar would raise a glass to Uncle Hector's memory while I stood there, beet-faced.

But instead, she slapped me on the shoulder, kissed me on the cheek, and shouted, "Well, ain't you a daisy! Helped yourself to Mr. P's clothes, did you?" Before I could reply, she added, "You hungry, puddin'? I know how boys are."

It struck me that if anybody would know about the appetites of men and boys, it would be the beauteous Belle, but I wisely kept my mouth shut and simply nodded a yes. After a word to Willie, she led me through the noisy crowd toward a small, unoccupied table beneath the stairs. Someone yelled a rather rude comment at her—something about robbing the cradle, although it was phrased far more indelicately—and she responded by shouting, "Aw, go suck an egg, Abner!"

I didn't get a chance to see who Abner was, because just then Belle shoved me between two tall gentlemen—one of whom I guessed to be an undertaker, because of his somber dress—and pushed me down into a chair. She plopped down opposite me, and with an arched brow, said, "Better?"

I assumed she meant better than shouldering our way through the throng, and nodded. This evening she was dressed more chastely than she had been earlier, if you could call anything ever worn by Belle chaste, and she appeared younger, closer to my age. I was beginning to fall for her, I suppose. Beginning? Part of me had already toppled.

I leaned toward her, looked into those big blue eyes, and said, "Why wasn't anyone sitting here?" The place was packed, but not a soul had so much as pulled out a chair at this table. I half expected that someone had sawn through the legs as a joke, and that any minute it would give way.

She cocked her head and pointed to her ear, and I asked again, this time shouting the question.

She grinned. "Mr. P's private table. Don't you fret

about this mob. Willie'll push 'em out by two. Here comes Ma!''

I looked up in time to see the approach of a napkin-covered tray, held high overhead, and then the woman beneath it, the same one who'd brought me the roast beef sandwich. Cowhands, gamblers, miners, and field hands alike parted before her like the Red Sea. I could see why. Just as grumpy-looking as before, she slid the tray to my table with a scowl.

"Thanks, Ma," shouted Belle.

Ma grunted and disappeared into the sea of bodies again.

I gulped. "Your mother?" I asked. I suppose I had some lunatic idea that I'd marry Belle, and that this cow would be my mother-in-law.

But Belle replied, "You fooling?" without further explanation, then added, "Eat up, kid."

With that, she was gone, leaving me to my tray and my thoughts, and the fifty-some bodies laughing and carousing and jostling the back of my chair.

Mother had once told me to chew every bite of my food thirty times, and since she had said so little—that I can recall, at any rate—I remembered her instruction and adhered to it. Thus, it was a good twenty-five minutes before I finished my meal, which turned out to be half a cold roast hen, nicely seasoned, with parsleyed new potatoes swimming in butter, green beans, and another slice of that good apple pie. This was accompanied by a large glass of buttermilk in addition to a bottle of sarsaparilla, although this time someone had dusted the bottle.

By the time I enthusiastically scraped my pie plate of every last crumb, Willie and his fellow bartenders had nearly emptied the place out. The music had stopped, and push brooms were already at work on the floor.

There had been at least a hundred bodies crowding the bar when I came downstairs, but at the moment, only three nonemployees remained. Two were slumped over tables and snoring peacefully. Another lay in the middle of the floor, his head centering a small pool of greenish-brown vomit. One grimy thumb was tucked into his mouth, and his chest slowly rose and fell. As I recall, he was smiling.

"Finally!" said Belle as she emerged from the curtained hall, next to the stage. She strode toward me, shapely legs flashing beneath her short, frothy skirt. "Thought we'd never get rid of 'em tonight."

As she pulled out a chair and settled in—and I wrested my eyes from her pretty dimpled knees—I asked, "What about them?" and pointed to the men at the tables and the one on the floor.

"Well, we usually leave 'em be till mornin', but we can pile 'em up outside on the walk if they're botherin' you," she replied, and raised an arm to beckon Willie.

"No, no," I said quickly. "Don't change anything on my account."

She shrugged. "You're the boss, kid."

"That's a laugh," announced Cole's voice. Startled, I twisted in my chair in time to see him step down off the last riser of that long staircase. He had changed and washed and shaved since I'd last seen him, but he still wore those pearl-handled pistols on his hips. He walked with a slight swagger, too.

Well, I shouldn't say it was exactly a swagger. It was more a thing of total ease in his body, a sort of artless grace. Everything about his body and manner said, "Watch out, you. I am a man to be reckoned with."

Everything about mine said, "I am a clumsy dolt. Kick me."

I suddenly found myself as envious of him as I was intimidated.

I wanted to crawl under the table and stay there until I was twenty-five.

But I sat up straight despite my inadequacies, knowing full well that to Belle—and likely everyone in the territory—I was nothing to this man. I was nothing to anyone, really, except maybe a few fellows at Tattinger's. I was prepared to be put firmly in my place.

I'd make him work for it, though. I was a Smith!

I said, "I don't know why that should strike you as humorous, sir. I am the proprietor now."

"On paper, maybe," Cole said. "Ownin' it and runnin' it's two different things." He pulled out a chair, turned it around backward with one move of his wrist, and eased himself down, his arms crossed over the back. "You got a name?"

I glanced over at Belle, and she said, "It's Horace, um . . . Horace . . ." My heart sank. She obviously didn't remember the rest of it, which knocked me down more pegs than Cole could possibly have done.

To top it off, Cole rolled his eyes and said, "Jesus."

Still, I said, "It's Horace Tate Pemberton Smith, sir." I believe I was a trifle testy. I know I was flustered.

"Yeah, that's it," Belle said with a nod.

"Well, don't go spreadin' it around," Cole growled, and signaled to Willie, who somehow knew that he wanted a beer and began to draw him one. "It'll get you laughed at or shot. Don't think you want either."

I took some umbrage at this, and began, "I don't see why—"

"Trust me, kid," he said.

I didn't reply.

"Now Tate's good," he went on. "I don't recall ever meetin' a Tate. You, Belle?"

"Well, there was Lambert Tate," she said with a toss of her pretty head. "He got himself hanged for thievin' chickens over toward Plano, Texas. And then there was Bob Tater, which is close, I mean the Tater part, but the last I heard he was down to Sonora, raisin' hell."

She was dressed in a sort of powder blue, and it did the most wonderful things for her eyes. I had already forgiven her for forgetting the whole of my name, and I was impressed—no, proud—that she could talk so calmly about a man who had been hanged for stealing chickens. She was so worldly!

"But I don't recall nobody with that for a first name, though," she finished up.

"Met a few Horaces," Cole said offhandedly. "Rubes and candy-ass greenhorns, the lot. The one that lived the longest was dead inside two weeks."

I had never heard the term "candy-ass greenhorn," but I feared it fit me to a tee.

"Tate," Belle said, and smiled. "I like that."

Suddenly, so did I. Then, I would have liked anything that Belle did. If she had liked short men, I would have run right out and had my feet chopped off. That's how smitten I was. I already had a change of location, I reasoned, so why not a change of name? It was still mine, or one of them, anyway. I was making a new start.

"Tate Smith," I said, rolling it around in my mouth, trying it out. It had a good feel to it, a nice bite. I believed I could get used to it.

"Your folks throw out the Donovan entirely?" Cole asked. "Would'a thought it'd be there somewhere in the middle."

I arched a brow. "I beg your pardon?"

Belle clucked her tongue and hissed, "Mayhap he don't know, Cole."

"Don't know what?" I asked, looking back and forth between the two of them.

"That your jackass daddy changed his name, boy," Cole said as his beer arrived. He took a long sip while I sat there, openmouthed, and then he added, "Didn't want anybody to know he was Irish. Can you beat that?"

"He certainly did not change it!" I said, leaning away. "My father was . . . was . . ." It occurred to me that I really had no idea who or what my father was, not really, and I stuttered to a stop. Lamely, I added, "He certainly wouldn't change his name."

Cole snorted. "Have it your own way, kid." He lifted his beer again.

Something about the accusation—and the demeanor in which it was delivered—made me more angry than the circumstances justified. But Cole was ignoring me now, and I returned the compliment. A change of subject was in order.

My face hot and my hands balled into fists beneath the table, I turned toward Belle. "I should like to see the books for this establishment. The mines, too. Perhaps tomorrow?"

"Sure thing, kid" had barely passed her lips when I could stand it no longer.

I twisted back toward Cole and nearly shouted, "Whyever would my father change his name?"

"Calm down, Horace," Belle soothed. "It's all right." She looked a tad alarmed.

"Told you," Cole said with a smirk. " 'Cause he

didn't want anybody to know he was one a' them high-strung Irishmen.''

I would have struck him if I hadn't been absolutely certain that he would gleefully pound me into pulp. So I unclenched my fists, gripped the edge of the table, and said, through gritted teeth, "I'll have you know, sir, that my father didn't have the slightest hint of the brogue on his tongue. His people were from London. They were all financiers. They were pillars of polite society!" I made those last three parts up, I admit. I had no real ammunition to throw.

Cole still had that smirk on his face, and Belle turned to him, whispering, "Why you gotta do this now, you sonofabitch?"

"Do what now?" I demanded. "Tell me lies?"

Belle caught my right hand in both of hers, and said, "Now, Horace—I mean, Tate, honey—Mr. P used to go on and on about it, you know? About how his only sister married a shanty Irishman . . . that is, an Irish feller—"

"Who didn't have the balls to own up to it," Cole cut in. "Never did know what was so consarned bad about bein' Irish in the first place," he muttered into his beer.

"Your daddy come over when he was a baby," Belle said. She was still hanging on to my hand for dear life, probably to keep me from hitting Cole. I was exceedingly glad for the excuse not to. "And his folks died when he was just a kid. And he did right good by himself, right good by you and your mama, didn't he? Even if he took a new moniker, I mean. It never bothered your mama—hell, he was a Smith before they ever met up, the way I heard—but Mr. P? That was a whole different colored bangtail, I can tell you!"

I felt as if somebody had let all the air out of me, and slumped back in my chair. Each new affront— my parents' deaths, the train, Uncle Horace, this den of lewd women and drunkards and, for all I knew, white slavery—seemed the final blow, but this topped them all. I wasn't even a Smith! I was a Donovan, and a member of a race that my father had always despised, or at least appeared to.

I could recall a time before I went away to school, when some of the silver came up missing. Father had dismissed pretty Miss Moira O'Hara without a reference, even though she was an upstairs maid and probably never got within twenty feet of the silver service, saying, "The filthy Irish. Thieves, every last one."

But he should have known, shouldn't he? I thought dismally. Aloysius Dean, his attorney, had mentioned something about father being deep in debt. I wished I had paid more attention.

I supposed that my father, the great Theodore Smith (nee Donovan), master of Wall Street and captain of industry, had been a thief, too. His pedestal, which had been slowly sinking into the mire since that fateful conversation with Misters Dean and Cummings, and which I had been trying to shoulder up ever since, had now dipped well below ground level, and Father already was up to his hips in the muck.

I stared down at the table and whispered, "I'm a *Donovan*?"

I heard Belle whisper, "Now you done it, you son-ofabitch. He's gone all flummoxy. Doggone you anyhow, Cole!"

4

I couldn't stand much more of this, I thought the next afternoon as I stared blankly at the so-called ledgers. Uncle Hector's bookkeeping system was beyond appalling, past cryptic, and into the realm of the surreal.

That, along with the collection of rusty Spanish bridle bits I had found in one of the dresser drawers—and a collection of cut-glass doorknobs that had toppled from a cupboard shelf and onto my still-aching head earlier in the day—had convinced me that although Uncle Hector had possessed good taste in clothing, he'd been one step away from the loony house.

I'd had doubts before, but I was quickly learning that everybody west of the Hudson was, well, crazy. Even Belle—who, I had to keep reminding myself, was a prostitute, a profession that couldn't be redeemed by her beauty—seemed a tad addled in the head at least some of the time. Asking me to change my name, of all things!

In the end, I had informed her that I would be referred to as Horace Smith, period, and that I was having none of this Tate Donovan business. Cole could go to the devil, so far as I was concerned.

I had decided the latter that morning. I had popped awake at seven on the dot, as usual, but found Hanratty's as silent as a tomb. After thinking it over, I'd gone back to bed and alternately dozed and puzzled over my situation until nearly noon, when the heat—and Uncle Hector's toppling doorknobs—drove me downstairs.

There would be no Tate Donovan, I thought as I rubbed the bumps on my head. My parents had named me Horace Tate Pemberton Smith, by God, and I was going to stick with it. The way things looked, that name might be the only thing I had left of them.

And this business about Father changing his name? Why, I only had Cole's word for that, didn't I?

Belle's, too, but that was beside the point.

Father might well have done it. He may well have been a thief, too. But he was my father, the only one I'd had, and if he'd been a thief, he'd at least been of the high-class variety. There was some comfort in that.

I convinced myself that Uncle Hector had some

sort of petty grudge against Father, perhaps no more than that he'd married Mother, and had spun the name-changing story out of all proportion.

And if someone was going to shoot me on account of such a piddling thing as a first name—a first name, I might add, that I had worn perfectly well up until last night—then let him pull the trigger.

So there.

And when you got right down to it, I had nowhere else to go. Uncle Hector's enterprises had landed squarely in my lap, and I intended to do as best as I could by them. I steeled myself to living in this insane asylum—although firmly in the role of keeper, not inmate—and see it through.

But now, as I sat in his office surrounded by all the paraphernalia I hadn't noticed the afternoon before—among them a collection of brass elephants and another of assorted rocks and minerals—I branded Uncle Hector with the immutable title of collector gone mad.

As I said, his books, to put in bluntly, were a catastrophe. More than half the time, in the place of numbers, he had entered arcane symbols or a little series of dots, or even tiny pictures of birds or reptiles or cacti. Sometimes they'd be all jumbled together, so that a line might read "7-duck-4-lizard-dot-dot-dot-snake." I could make neither heads nor tails of it. So desperate was I that I even tried turning the books to a mirror, a trick I'd gleaned from one of Clive's auxiliary accumulation of mystery books.

It didn't help.

The ledgers for the mines were in much the same shape as those for Hanratty's, although they were far slimmer. I couldn't make sense of them, either. Nobody could have, except perhaps Uncle Hector, and I had my doubts about that.

I had no idea where we stood on anything. I searched through the desk drawers and turned up nothing more interesting than a stack of receipts for whiskey, beer, and bar supplies, another stack for foodstuffs, and one that was a jumble of bills marked PAID for everything from lamp oil to French letters to quicksilver to silk stockings.

Uncle Hector might have been as mad as a hatter, but at least he was a prompt-paying madman. I'd give him that.

I called for Willie, who after some difficulty helped me locate the combination to the wall safe. Inside it, I found a few things of note. The deed to Hanratty's and the land upon which it stood, for one thing. It appeared to be free of encumbrances, and for this, I was grateful.

An envelope disclosed the deeds to the three mines Belle had mentioned: the sole proprietorship in the Aztec Princess and the Lucky Seven, and half ownership in the Two Bit, the other half being owned by someone named Lop Ear Tommy Cleveland.

The records for each girl were in there, too, plus those for Ma and the bartenders. These, thankfully, were much more straightforward than the books for the saloon, being written entirely with actual numbers, and in English instead of hieroglyphs. There was a page for each girl: how much she had taken in on a day-by-day basis, and what she had been paid.

There seemed to be a great deal of money in whoremongering.

But the most interesting thing I found inside the safe was contained in a very small but exceedingly heavy cardboard box. It was another stone, but not like the collection of rocks and minerals displayed on the desk and side tables.

I gasped, I think. At least, I sat down hard in Uncle Hector's chair.

It was an igneous rock, seemingly chiseled fresh from the earth. I remembered that much—the igneous part, I mean—from Mr. Case's geology class. The thing was roughly square, and on two sharply cleaved sides, it showed pale milky quartz tinged with pink. That wasn't the thing that had me sitting on the edge of my chair though, for right in the middle of that quartz, there was a thick vein of gold.

At least, I was fairly certain it was gold. I could have kicked myself for not paying more attention in class! The whole of the stone—from the rough rock exterior covering most of it to the quartz with its astonishing contents—was smaller than a hen's egg, yet far heavier than it should have been.

Gold was heavy, wasn't it? But then, perhaps fool's gold was, too. Mr. Case had shown us some of that— pyrite, I think it was called—but that had been in shiny little metal crystals, and this certainly was neither shiny nor crystalized. It looked as if it had been poured into a channel in the rock millions of years ago, when the earth was new and the rock was molten.

Trembling, I slapped my pockets until I found my penknife. Afraid to set the stone down lest it should vanish into thin air, I managed to pry open the knife with my teeth and press the blade, hard, into the precious metal.

It left a small dent.

I dropped my knife to the desk and hugged that rock to my heart for a period of perhaps fifteen seconds, until reality took hold of me. It was gold, all right, but hardly a monumental sum.

But why had Uncle Hector locked it away instead of displaying it with his other rocks and minerals? After all, there was a chunk of milky quartz eight times the size of this sitting right in front of me. That one contained black streaks of raw silver, a large protrusion of which had been worked and polished to a sheen. Uncle Hector had been using it for a paperweight.

"Snoopin'? You been busy."

I looked up to see Cole standing in the doorway, and for moment I felt horribly guilty. But then I remembered who I was, sat up a little straighter, and said, "I'd hardly call it snooping, sir."

"Knock that 'sir' shit off, kid," he said, and slouched down in the chair I'd sat in while Belle told me about Uncle Hector's death. Cole glanced at the open safe, then the empty box, and then nodded toward my hands, which still clutched the ore to my vest. "Found it, huh?"

I tilted my head. "Found what? And I'd appreciate it if you'd stop calling me 'kid.' Horace will do, thank you."

He ignored all but my first sentence, replying, "Heck's gold." When I didn't answer, he grunted and added, "Jesus. You can stop hidin' it. I seen it before."

"Seen what before?" said a voice from the hall. Belle stepped into the doorway. She grinned, and I believe I sighed. My thoughts of her, it seemed, were stern only when she wasn't in my presence.

But Cole kept his eyes leveled on me and said, "Go away, honey. Me and the kid got things to talk over."

He was really beginning to irritate me. I began, "I told you before, please don't call me—"

"Sure, sugar," interrupted Belle. "You eat, darlin'?" she asked me with a bat of her lashes.

"Thank you, yes," I replied. "Willie was kind enough to—"

"What you got there?" she interrupted, pointing to my clasped hands.

"Get, Belle," Cole snapped. "Now."

That pretty smile turned into a prettier scowl. "You're 'bout as fun as a singed wolverine this mornin', Cole," she grumbled as she pulled the door closed between us, then slammed it the last two inches. The etched glass in the door rattled.

Cole, who had not taken his eyes from mine during the entire conversation, parroted, "Sir and ma'am, please and thank you." He was not smiling. "You're just about too goddamn polite to live—you know that?"

"And you, sir, are becoming an annoyance," I said sternly.

I had never in my life spoken to a grown person in this manner, and the moment the words left my lips I was torn between apologizing and crowing.

Oddly enough, Cole didn't seem to notice the difference. "You tryin' to push that rock out the other side of you?"

I realized I was still clutching the ore to my chest, and reluctantly set it on the desk. I pointed at it. "You say you've seen this before?" I asked, arrogance fairly dripping from my voice. "Is it your habit to go through my uncle's safe?"

"You know where it came from, boy?"

"The safe, of course!" The man was an idiot.

He leaned back in his chair, rolled his eyes, and said, "Fine. Never mind. But I'd put it back in there if I was you. Won't pay none to flash it around."

As much as I would have liked to leave it out, if for no other reason than to vex him, I snatched up the rock, put it back in its little cardboard box, and returned it to the safe.

"Happy?" I asked.

"Overjoyed," he said dryly, and yawned. "Can't you tell? See you been goin' through Heck's books. You make anything outta them pig squiggles?"

"No," I said, sitting down again. It did no good to get angry at a man who didn't seem to care. Or even notice. I made a conscious effort to tamp down my irritation. And also, to glean what information I could from him. "I haven't a clue."

"Same here. Ol' Heck was real secretive 'bout his books and things."

"So it would seem." I hadn't yet come across anything to tell me whether I was about to sink to the bottom of the financial sea or not. The filing cabinets might hold something, but there were four of them with four drawers each. Daunting, at best. I'd be looking until Christmas, and even then, I'd likely find nothing more than what Cole called Uncle Hector's pig squiggles.

But Cole had obviously seen the books, even looked in the safe. It occurred to me, somewhat belatedly, that Cole might know how Uncle Hector had been financially fixed.

A slight hitch in my voice, I began, "Would you know . . . is there a bank account?" I had come across nothing that even vaguely resembled a bankbook.

"Sure," he said, with no hesitation. "Two of 'em. Doubt if there's more than a hundred bucks betwixt 'em, though. Heck pumped near everything he had into the mines. Well, just the one, lately. Mines're awful pricey hobbies, kid, and they sucked every penny out of Hanratty's. More'n once he's had to ask your daddy for a stake.''

"Pardon?''

"Money to get a new one up and runnin'.''

"Oh, marvelous,'' I said with what I am afraid was a little wail, and dropped my head into my hands. Uncle Hector was broke and dead, Father was in the same condition, and I was halfway there. At least I was keeping with family tradition.

But then it occurred to me that by itself, without the drain of Uncle Hector's hobbies and eccentricities, Hanratty's might do quite splendidly. It didn't appear to be in debt. At least Uncle Hector had died solvent—technically speaking, at any rate. That was more than I could say for Father. And as to the moral dilemma of renting out scantily clad soiled doves by the hour, well, I'd deal with that later.

"These mines of Uncle Hector's,'' I said, slowly raising my head until I met Cole's eyes once again. "Are these other two—the Aztec Princess and the Two Bit, I mean—worth anything? The land?''

Cole shrugged. He had lit a cigarette, and it dangled from one corner of his mouth.

"I should like to inspect them.''

He stared at me with no change of expression.

Well, he likely wouldn't be pleasant company, but he was the best that was handy, and I was in a hurry. I swallowed my pride completely. "Would you . . . would you consider accompanying me?''

Slowly, he sat forward and took the cigarette from his lips. "All you had to do was ask, kid."

He rose, ground his smoke out on Uncle Hector's polished floor—my floor—and said, "Well, we'd best get you outfitted. It's a long ride. And you'd damn well better not be as tender as you look."

We made a stop at the bank, and I learned with some satisfaction that Cole had been wrong about the money. There was more than a paltry hundred dollars in Uncle Hector's accounts. There was a total of two hundred and twenty-four dollars and thirty-seven cents, to be exact.

However, since the Lucky Seven mine also had access to the business account—and since Cole told me that it had been producing barely enough copper to break even—I left those funds alone. I instructed Willie and Belle to deposit all profits from Hanratty's into that account, also. They were still digging Uncle Hector out of the Lucky Seven, after all, and I had a feeling that the exhumation would prove expensive.

I just hoped they were digging up a little copper while they were at it.

I took fifteen dollars from Uncle Hector's personal account. This, when added to the last of my travel money and a portion of the petty cash from the till at Hanratty's, was enough to outfit me for ten days' worth of roughing it on the open plain, and leave twelve dollars cash in my pocket.

When we left the mercantile, loaded with gear, I

was wearing a brand-new Colt Peacemaker on my hip. Cole had insisted I'd need it, and despite the fact that it cost me dear, I didn't need much coaxing before it topped my pile of purchases.

Oh, it was a beautiful thing, a precision instrument! It wasn't so fancy as Cole's pearly eagle butts, but it was heavy and solid and shiny and quite deadly-looking, with ornate etchings on the barrel and ebony grips. Cole loaded it with five cartridges, firmly instructing me to keep the hammer on the empty chamber.

"Be just like a greenhorn to shoot off his own damn knee," he grumbled.

We dropped my purchases off at Hanratty's, which was by this time open for business. There was a fight going on in the back corner, near the stage. I started to move toward it—to do exactly what, I had no idea—but Cole caught my shoulder.

"It's just them Fisk brothers again," he said, as one cracked a bottle over the other's head. The bottle broke and the crackee staggered, but didn't go down. "Willie'll see it don't get too serious."

It looked pretty serious to me already. There was quite a bit of blood involved, at any rate, but nobody seemed terribly upset, save the two combatants. To the sound of the man with the bleeding head breaking a chair over his brother's back, Cole and I left Hanratty's and made our way to the livery stable.

This was more for Cole's benefit than mine, because he bought a horse. I soon learned, to my great delight, that I already had one—another hand-me-down from Uncle Hector—and I fussed over him while Cole dickered with a couple of mustachioed horse traders.

Tellurium was my mount's name, and he was a sleek gray gelding, well conformed and roughly fifteen hands, with a silvery sheen to his dappled coat. He had a black mane and tail, making him very flashy, I thought, with clean, sound limbs, and large, well-spaced eyes, which gave every indication of a gentle nature.

When I asked Cole what the horse's name meant, thinking it might be the name of a local politician or a Western hero of some sort, he shrugged. "Some kinda rock, I think."

Leave it to Uncle Hector. I considered myself lucky that he hadn't trained the horse to commands in Aramaic or ancient Sumarian. Then it occurred to me that he might have done just that, so I took hold of Tellurium's halter and said, "Back, Tellurium, back."

He backed up a few steps, and I said, "Good fellow."

Tellurium proved a mouthful inside five minutes, however. I straightened his forelock, ran my hands over his neck and withers, and said, "I shall call you Tell, then. What do you say to that?"

.He snorted softly. I took it for a yes.

I will admit something to you. When I saw that horse and learned he was mine, all mine to keep, my

eyes flooded with tears until I had to turn away so
Cole couldn't see.

My mount at Tattinger's, Cavalier, had been just a
stable horse, true, but I had been terribly fond of him.
I'd ridden him exclusively since I'd first enrolled, and
out of all the things I missed about school, I think I
missed him the most. When Tell rubbed his broad
forehead against me, then lipped at my pockets, looking for carrots or sugar, it was the first true sense of
"home" that I'd had.

"You and me, Tell," I whispered to him in that
stall. "Us, forever." I meant it, too.

Cole argued with the traders for over an hour, and
finally settled on a handsome dark bay gelding
named Ranger, with two white socks behind, and a
snip and a star. I thought this was strange. Not the
horse, mind, but that Cole had to buy him at all.

When I asked why he was purchasing Ranger—I
thought that every Westerner owned a mount, for
goodness' sake!—he scowled at me and said, "Why
you figure I come back to town on the damn stage,
boy, with my saddle and gear tied up top? Some yellow bastard shot the sonofabitch out from under me."

"*What?*" I asked, shocked to my soul that anyone
would shoot a horse for no reason, let alone while a
man was riding him! "When?"

"When I was up seein' about Heck," he snapped
and led Ranger out to the paddock, effectively halt-
ing the conversation.

5

We rode out of Tonto's Wickiup early the next morning, after a tearful farewell from Belle—which I admit was delivered entirely to Cole, not me—and after Ma wordlessly shoved a parcel at me, then stomped back inside.

"Give it here," Cole said gruffly as he snatched it away and tucked it into his bulging saddlebag.

"Who *is* that woman?" I asked as we jogged south, down the ragged main street and out of town. I was having some trouble with my stirrups.

"Shorten your leathers a notch" was all he said.

We were past the fringes of town before I got my stirrups even—a clumsy thing to attempt when you're trying to ride at the same time—and by that time I had forgotten all about Ma. I was full of youthful fervor about the journey. The thought of rattlesnakes and the like—not to mention the realities of camping in the wilderness—cast a bit of a pall over the proceedings, but were not enough to dampen my spirits.

I would see this country firsthand, and not just from the enclosure of a speeding stagecoach or train. I would inspect the mines, and then I would sell them to the highest bidder. I would have quite a tale to tell Clive Barrow, who I hadn't got around to writing yet.

Additionally, this would be my first true step toward taking charge, toward actually doing something that would affect my own future. Having been thrust into a grown-up world, I intended to make the most of it.

I wished I had slept better the night before, though. Between my anxiety over the trip and the noise from downstairs, I managed to get a total of two and a half hours before Cole came banging on my door at five. I was running on nerves and Ma's coffee, of which I had downed three strong cups.

However, I was not so enthusiastic about Cole's company as I was about my new gun, or my new hat, or my new leather chaps. He had done little but grouse and complain—or worse, kept irritatingly silent—for the whole of the time we were making our purchases. Frankly, I was torn between admiration for the man and wanting to throttle him.

He was certainly well-versed in the ways of the wild country, or at least seemed to be. I didn't really know that I was one to judge. But I watched him carefully, and as I rode along behind him, I gave wide berth to the same cacti he did, aped the low tilt of his hat, and watched the way that the top and bottom halves of his body seemed to move independently of each other. It was entirely graceful, and I tried to emulate it. His was a far different equestrian posture than I had been taught, and it took a while to get the hang of it, but it seemed, well, more comfortable.

I daresay my riding master at Tattinger's would have given me a stern dressing down if he had seen me, though.

We stopped every so often to rest and water the horses, and I soon saw why Cole had insisted we bring along so much water. Our horses were loaded with the stuff, both in canteens and large canvas bags, which sweated and dripped continuously and kept both my knees damp.

Most of the time, we kept to a walk or a very slow trot to which I didn't have to post—and which Cole, in a rather derisive tone, was quick to inform me was called a "jog"—mainly on account of the water's extra weight.

Cole said very little to me, either while we rode or when we stopped. I noticed that he glanced me over at each rest, as if he were looking for a weakness of some sort that he could exploit, but he rarely said more than "Loosen your girth, kid" or "Hand me that jerky."

I was too goggle-eyed at the scenery and too thirsty to instigate further conversation.

Now about the jerky. This was a food I'd never seen before, and once I tasted it, I hoped never to see it again. It was meat, or so they claimed—dry, tough, relentlessly chewy, and for the most part tasteless. I finally broke down and asked, "How the devil do they make this wretched foodstuff?"

He said, with a perfectly straight face, "They butcher a goat and nail it to a tin roof for a week." And then he studied for a moment on the chunk he was eating, said, "Maggot," and plucked off a little piece of something.

I felt the last swallow of water I'd taken rising up my throat, but managed to hold it back. I dropped the jerky I'd been gnawing into the low scrub behind my back, though. Maggots! I grabbed my canteen and downed half of it, just to get the imagined taste of filthy carrion bugs out of my mouth.

Cole smiled a little too smugly and said, "Cinch him up again, Tate. Daylight's wastin'."

"Don't call me Tate," I growled as I tightened Tell's girth. It was the second time that day he'd called me by that name.

He swung a leg over Ranger. "All right, Donovan," he said, and started out again.

Honestly, I wanted to punch him for calling me that. I would have if he hadn't been far ahead by the time I mounted Tell, and I might have gotten in one or two good swings before he flattened me. After all, I'd been on the boxing team at Tattinger's until I turned all knees and elbows. I wasn't sure exactly how much credence Cole would put into the Marquis of Queensbury rules, though.

Shadows were growing long, there was a pinkish cast to the horizon, and my backside felt like a well-pounded steak. The first all-day stint in the saddle is rough on the most seasoned rider, even when he has a fine, soft-gaited mount, such as my Tell.

I'd had my fill of endless vistas, soaring eagles and hawks, darting quail, and skulking coyotes for the day, and for the past half hour, I had been half-expecting—no, actually praying a little—that Cole would call a halt to the proceedings. So when he reined in Ranger and sat there for a moment, waiting for me to catch him up, I breathed a small sigh of relief. I wanted nothing more than to stand on solid ground again, and I wanted to stand on it for a good deal longer than fifteen or twenty minutes.

But once I rode up beside him, he turned to me and said, "You're pretty fair on the mosey, kid. I'll give you that. Let's see what you can really do."

And with that, he dug his heels into Ranger and sped away.

I was so surprised that it took me a second or two to realize that I was supposed to follow him, that this was some kind of idiot frontier test. My Tell was game and eager for the chase though. He half-reared, I gave him his head, and we thundered after.

We were gaining on Cole before I knew it! Out of

habit, I crouched low on Tell's neck, moving my weight forward over his withers, balancing in stirrups that still felt too long. All my reservations vanished in a twinkling, though.

Tell's dark mane slapped at my face. The wind pushed at my hat and I held it on with one hand. It was like flying, and I was laughing, actually laughing!

I saw Cole briefly turn to see if I was still following. I think he was surprised that I'd gained at least four lengths on him, and was at that moment within two of him. He cut to the left, around a thick clump of cactus, and barreled straight toward what appeared to be a sharp drop-off.

I was enjoying myself too much to stop, let alone question his path. As nimble as a rabbit, Tell followed him around the cactus, across the flat, and then down the incline. It was a perilous slope, and I was on it and sliding down before I knew it. The instant that Tell started down, I clenched my teeth, tightened my reins so that I had contact with his mouth, and prayed that he'd make it to the bottom without killing us both.

But oh, he was nimble!

Skidding and hopping in a manner that would have been the end of any rangy prep school hunter, we reached the bottom after what felt like five minutes—but was probably only a few seconds—to find Cole waiting for us with a smirk on his face.

I rode up to him, anger having replaced my previous exhilaration, and shouted, "Are you crazy? You could have killed us!" I jumped off Tell to check his legs for cuts. That slope had been rocky.

I found no abrasions, thank God.

"You did good, kid," Cole said calmly. "Guess they taught you how to ride back east, after all."

I stuck my foot back in Tell's stirrup. "You thought I'd lie to you?" I huffed in irate disbelief. "If you were going to put me through some kind of moronic test, why didn't you do it earlier, when the horses were fresh?"

"Too much water weight," he said, without a change in expression. "They drunk almost half of it by now." He reined Ranger away and started down the draw I had just realized we were in.

I rode up beside him. "Cole, I don't think I like you very much at the moment." I scraped sweat off Tell's pale silver neck with the flat of my hand, then flicked it to the ground.

"You don't gotta like me, kid. I'm doin' this mine thing for Heck. And I done that"—he pointed over his shoulder, toward the path our free-for-all race had taken—"to find out just what kind of pluck you had."

"Pluck? *Pluck?* You nearly killed my horse—not to mention me—to find out if I had pluck? Are you mad, sir?"

"Been accused of worse," he said. "And I'da only killed you. That horse you're ridin' is one tough old brush popper." He rode on.

Once the horses had cooled out, the sunset had

nearly passed, and the sky had gone to deep purple tinged with orange, Cole finally stopped and we made camp.

I had expected a roaring fire and a cozy tent, but instead I got a feeble blaze just big enough to heat coffee. That, and a blanket on the ground. We took care of the horses and I got my bedding laid out, all in silence, and then Cole tossed me my rope. I caught it and stood there, staring at him.

"Ring your pallet, Donovan," he said.

I had halfway calmed down from that impromptu race, but this stoked my fires again. "If you don't stop calling me that, I will have to take measures, sir!"

"I'll think about it, soon as you stop callin' me sir. Now ring your bed with that rope."

"Why?"

"Snakes."

I think I sucked in a good bit of air. "Snakes?" I asked weakly, and immediately looked down at my feet and the ground around me. Would snakes be brave enough to venture so near the fire?

Cole wasn't watching me, though. He was spreading a loop around his own sleeping place.

Quite conversationally, he said, "Now some fellers say the little hairs on the rope tickles their bellies, and they don't like that. Some'll tell you the rattlers think it's another snake, and that's why they don't cross. Me?" he said, straightening up again. "I just figure whatever works works."

I got busy with my rope.

For our dinner, we delved into Ma's mystery package. There was an entire chicken, cut up and fried, which was delicious, plus hard-boiled eggs—enough to last for several days—and a few small, wizened oranges. Shriveled or not, these last were a real delicacy after a day in the heat. I don't believe that I had ever sweated so much—or downed so much water—in one day.

While we ate, I pondered how in the world to broach the subject that I'd been trying, to no avail, to open with Cole. Namely, why he believed Uncle Hector might have met with foul play. This was more difficult than you might suspect, because I'd overheard the conversation, and a gentleman never admits to eavesdropping.

Well, to put a finer point on it, a gentleman never eavesdrops in the first place.

But in the end, I didn't ask, not that night. It seemed so complicated, and I was so bleary-eyed and weary—and yes, sore—that the moment I swallowed the last of my second orange I fell asleep, still clutching the peel in my fingers.

"We're here," Cole announced.

It was roughly two o'clock in the afternoon, and as far as I could tell, we were in the middle of nowhere. Low, rocky, gravelly hills had replaced the flatland of yesterday, and the vegetation, while sparser, was no more interesting.

The only things to set this landscape off from what we'd been riding through for the past four or five hours were a couple of widely spaced pits, for lack of a better term, each only a few feet across.

I couldn't tell how deep they went, but I thought they were awfully big for animal dwellings. An army of badgers, all denned together? A vast family of coyotes?

"We're where, exactly?" I asked, craning my head back and forth, and hoped that a phalanx of mountain lions wouldn't suddenly emerge from one of those holes and come barreling toward us, fangs bared.

He stepped down from Ranger, then took off his hat and wiped his brow on the back of his sleeve. "Aztec Princess," he said as he led the horse away from me.

"Where?" I repeated. I stood up in my stirrups, but there was still no sign announcing that this was the Aztec Princess, not even a remnant of one. No miners' quarters, no stamping mill. No mine, period.

I gave Tell a little nudge with my knees, and rode up beside Cole, who had pulled down his last water bag but was still on foot, leading Ranger.

"Would you care to explain yourself, sir?" I asked, trying not to sound too huffy.

He stopped and looked up at me. "I'd get off that nag if I was you, Donovan."

I opened my mouth to say something utterly cutting, but before I could, he added, "They tunneled too close to the surface in more'n a few places. Best spread out your weight and the horse's lest you find another and fall through." He pointed toward a pit to my left, and repeated, "Get down. Now."

I still hadn't seen any mine shaft, but Cole sounded serious and I grudgingly dismounted. He snagged Tell's reins from my hands and nodded toward the pit. "Go and take a look if you don't believe me."

"Fine," I said. "I shall. And don't call me Donovan."

He grunted and led the horses off, toward the feeble shade.

I grunted right back at him, although I doubt that he heard me, and set out to have a look in this pit of his, thinking that if something fanged or clawed or hoofed boiled up out of it and attacked me, I would take my chances and try to thrash Cole.

Provided I survived the animal onslaught, of course.

But when I reached its edge, all my tenuous bravado fled. There, perhaps twenty feet below, was what remained of a wagon. And worse, the remains of a horse. Nothing but bones, harness fragments, rusted rims and broken wheels, and timbers all jumbled together like a jigsaw puzzle waiting to be worked.

I swallowed, hard.

The hapless creature had fallen through the roof of a tunnel, all right, wagon and all. The north end of the pit was blocked with debris, but I could just glimpse the opening that went south. Something alive scuttled beneath the skeleton's rib cage.

"Get back from the edge, you horse's butt!" Cole shouted.

I jumped back just as a little spray of gravel, right where my boot had been, sifted over the rim and spattered the bones below.

For once, I didn't correct Cole. I probably was a horse's butt.

Walking carefully, I joined him. He had already unsaddled Ranger, and was sitting in the shade at the base of yet another of those seemingly endless low hills, rolling himself a smoke.

"Is this safe?" I asked. My eyes were darting every which way, looking for shifting earth.

Cole snorted. "If you mean, are there any tunnels under us? No."

"There was a horse down there."

"Mule, actually. They got the other three out without a scratch." When I stared at him, he shrugged and added, "Heck liked to tell about it. Over and goddamn over again."

I shifted from foot to foot. "This is very interesting, I'm sure, but would you mind telling me where the mine is? The entrance, I mean."

He thumbed back his hat. "You're standin' thirty feet from it."

"Where?"

"There," he said, and pointed with the hand that held his tobacco pouch.

Even when my eye was directed to it, it took a second to see the thing: an opening in the hillside, low and camouflaged with planks the same dusty color as the clay and gravel of the ground. Also, a bush of some sort had grown up in front of it, so I think I can be excused.

"Ah," I said.

"Ah, indeed," said Cole, lighting his cigarette.

I scowled at him, although being busy with his smoke and match, he didn't see me. Was there ever a more maddening man?

"Well?" I asked.

He tossed his match to the ground. "Well, we're here. Do what you want. I ain't goin' nowhere." He drew deeply on his cigarette, and exhaled a yellowish plume. "If you're smart, you'll take yourself a little siesta." He leaned back, propping himself on an elbow, and proceeded to ignore me.

I should have hired somebody in town, I thought as I stripped Tell of his tack. I should have hired a complete stranger. At least he would have been civil, if only to get his pay.

That stranger would have called me Horace—no, Mr. Smith! He would have warned me about that jumping cholla I'd ridden too close to earlier in the morning. Oh, Cole had said something about it, but only when I was mumbling curses and picking spines out of Tell's legs.

By the time I'd given Tell a drink and put his hobbles on, Cole had finished his smoke and was flat on his back on the ground, his hat pulled low over his eyes.

So much for you, I thought. I pulled a candle and matches from my pack, stuffed the gloves Cole had made me buy in a back pocket, and set off toward the mine entrance.

But when I got there, I didn't immediately start ripping down boards. Something caught my eye, something about forty yards to the west.

The weather had muted their color and half-covered their forms in sand and grit, but I could see a few broken boards peeking from the brush. And beside them, jutting up behind a clump of brush and perhaps twenty feet away, there was a rusted pump handle.

Long ago, someone had dug a well, and there might even have been a building. Still, it didn't bode the best for me. I hardly thought there would be resale money in this property. No one in his right mind would want to live here, and I couldn't see that there had been decent grazing for even one lonely steer in the last five miles we'd traveled.

Oh, well. As long as we were here.

The place had been boarded up chockablock. Raw planks were nailed willy-nilly to other planks, so that the thing resembled something organic rather than man-made. It took me a moment to figure out where to start.

Glumly, I settled on a board, tugged on my gloves, and prepared to pry. The plank came away easily, the wood being brittle and the nails nearly rusted through. The second came just as readily, and the third, but I had trouble with the fourth. Upon closer inspection, I saw why.

New nails, still shiny once the dust was brushed away, secured it. The board was new, too. I frowned. Someone had entered the Aztec Princess, and quite recently. Several new pieces of lumber were tacked over the lower-right-hand part of the opening, in fact, and the bush that covered them appeared to have been transplanted there.

None too well, either, for it was dying. When I moved the lower branches away, the ground directly below it showed the marks where boots had stomped mud that had dried hard and brittle.

Curious.

I thought about calling for Cole, but a quick look showed him still stretched out and breathing deeply. I'd do this on my own.

I worked to the left, ripping down jury-rigged older planks, and soon opened a hole big enough to climb through.

I took the candle from my back pocket, lit it, and stepped inside.

6

The Aztec Princess wasn't exactly the best place to be alone.

Within five minutes of creeping along the disused main shaft—littered with fallen rock, webbed here and there by spiders spinning up fat roaches and crickets—I found myself wanting company, any company. Even Cole's. But pride can be strong in a young man, especially a foolish one, so I girded my loins and kept on.

To tell the truth, I really had no idea what I was looking for. Oh, silver, I suppose, but how would I be able to spot silver ore? Men far more seasoned than I had claimed to have mined it all and gone home. Within ten minutes, I had talked myself into believing I was on a fool's errand—which, in fact, I was. Cole, asleep up there in the purple shade, had known it all along.

I was angry at him for riding out here with me and thus fueling my hopes, angry at myself for thinking I might find something of value. The land was completely worthless. Any fool could see that.

I'd probably have to pay someone to take it off my hands.

But at this point, my fears—despite the spiders, the scurrying lizards, the squeaking rodents just beyond the range of my candle's light, and my intermittent "collywobbles," as Clive Barrow used to quip—my excursion had taken on something of a heady quality. There was something to be said for exploring, and a small thrill in discovery, even if you only found the occasional rusted chisel.

Within a half hour the whole business was beginning to pale, however, and I was wondering if I wasn't lost. I was about to turn and retrace my steps—or at least, I certainly hoped to—when I saw light up ahead, dusty and dim. Could I have come all the way back to the entrance and not noticed? I hardly thought so, even though I had lost all sense of direction and there had been several turns and twists and an abundance of side tunnels.

But I crept forward, closer to the light, holding my candle at an angle so the wax wouldn't drip on my hand. I had a wrist- and cuff-full already.

The light wasn't the entrance. It was another of those caved-in places. Not the one I'd peered into from above, for this one was far deeper than the first, being a good twenty-five feet from the top of the cave-in debris to the surface.

Also, it contained no mule's skeleton, only the remains of a freight wagon, half covered with detritus.

I was standing well back in the tunnel, puzzling over how in the world they ever got the mules out, when something stirred in the rubble. Something big.

Gooseflesh raced up my spine, and I took a step back. My candle shook.

"W-who's there?" I asked, like an idiot.

At the sound of my voice, amplified by the shaft, a dusty board exploded upward with a shower of dust motes. Something screamed.

I bolted.

I ran hard and fast back up the shaft, my heart pounding louder than my bootsteps, barely retaining the presence of mind to shield my candle's flame as I pounded onward. I wasn't sure that the screeching thing was still coming, but I didn't want to waste even a split second looking over my shoulder.

And in my rush to escape that which I was convinced was a mountain lion, possibly several, I took a wrong turn. I tripped headlong over an old barrel and straight into a muddy wall, and knocked myself unconscious.

"Don't move, kid" was the next thing I heard. It was Cole's voice, couched in a whisper. "Don't twitch so much as a finger—you hear me?"

My head ached, there was something poking me in the back, and my arm was twisted beneath me at a most uncomfortable angle. I croaked out, "Why-ever not?"

Immediately, there was a new sound, much too close. A sound like steam exiting a pipe under pressure.

"Don't talk, dammit," Cole hissed.

I opened my eyes. I could see Cole now, standing a few feet away. He held a flickering candle in one hand and his rifle in the other. "Don't even think about takin' a deep breath. You've got a rattler roostin' on your belly."

I gasped—I think anyone would have—and the hissing sound increased in volume. I cannot describe the fear that coursed through me, save to say that my bladder instantly emptied of its own accord, and the hand beneath my body tightened into a fist.

I held still, though.

I have said that I was lying in an awkward position, but when I got up the nerve to look down my nose, I could just see the top coil of the snake and his head above it. I could feel his weight then, too, shifting heavy and sinuous upon my shirt and trousers. Cole waved the tip of his rifle near the snake's face, and when it shifted position and struck at the barrel, I nearly screamed.

"Don't," Cole warned through clenched teeth.

He was lucky I wasn't vomiting.

Cole waved the rifle again. I saw the candle's flame

glint off the end of it just before the snake actually found his target. The rattler's strike was like lightning, and it clung to the tip of the rifle's barrel for perhaps a second before it let go. The thing immediately recoiled on my belly, ready for the next onslaught.

Cole took a step back, muttered, "Shit," and turned the rifle's barrel toward him. He studied it in the light of his candle. *What are you doing?* I wanted to shout. *Checking the blasted metal for damage?*

"Lookin' for venom," he said quietly, as if he were reading my thoughts. Or at least, part of them. "Can't shoot him without bringin' the roof down on us or blastin' a hole through you. Mayhap I can milk the poison out of him. Got a few drops that last time."

On the edge of hysterics, I thought, *Oh, marvelous. Just champion.*

If the serpent bit me, perhaps I wouldn't completely die. Perhaps I'd just have convulsions, run a fever of a hundred ten, permanently lose my mental capacities, and spend the rest of my life drooling quietly in some asylum.

How comforting.

Cole set his feet and swung the rifle out once more, teasing until, with a sudden, nauseating flex of muscle, the beast struck again.

This time, he didn't wait for the snake to release. In a split second he jerked the rifle to the side and up, taking the snake partway with it until its fangs slid off the metal. Then, almost faster than I could see, nearly as fast as the snake had struck, he flipped the rifle about and brought the stock of it down on the snake, close to the beast's head, to pin it against the wall. Quickly, he set the candle on a barrel, trading it for a good-sized rock I hadn't known he'd had in his pocket, and brought it down savagely on the snake's head.

I lay there, too terrified to move, while he bent over and picked up the still-writhing body. He stood for a moment, holding it out, and then he said, "Big one. Been eatin' fat ol' mine rats for a good long time. You know, you didn't have to go to all this fuss just to rustle us up some grub, kid."

For all I had wanted to say before, I found myself wordless, with only a sour taste in my mouth.

He leaned his rifle carefully on the keg that held his candle, and held down his hand. The one without the snake in it, I mean. It had only just stopped rattling.

"Anything busted?" he asked as he helped me up. "Besides your bladder, that is."

Heat raced up my neck. "No, sir," I said in a cracked voice. I was careful to stand on the other side of him, away from that wretched snake. The horrid thing was still twitching. "How long have I been . . . I mean, how long . . . ?"

"Been lookin' for you for 'bout a half hour," he said without meeting my eyes. "It's nigh on five."

"Five?" I said. It couldn't have been three when I

first entered the mine. I had spent some time walking, but I must have been unconscious for better than two hours. *You never do anything by halves, do you, Horace?* I thought.

"Here," he said, and thrust that filthy snake at me. "Hold this. You're damn lucky he didn't set up shop inside your pants leg."

I held the snake for perhaps two seconds, and then it twitched in a great spasm, coiling over my wrist. I dropped it to the ground, bloody and squashed head first, as a wave of nausea swept through me.

Cole wasn't paying the slightest bit of attention, though. He had moved forward to stand where I'd been lying. I now saw that we were in a dead-ended tunnel, perhaps no more than eight feet in length. By the looks of the debris that had been cast into it— empty crates, a few rusted shovels, the empty powder keg I'd tripped over plus several more, and so on—it had been the storage closet of choice for the workers.

Cole was holding the candle high, staring at the wall. Water was seeping in from somewhere. It left a faint, damp sheen on the left side of the wall. I hadn't the slightest idea where it was coming from, but perhaps this was the reason the miners hadn't pursued this particular shaft any further.

The dead snake, still wriggling obscenely, bumped against my boot, and I jumped. Telling myself in no uncertain terms that it had gone to its Maker and couldn't bite me—and besides, I doubted that Cole's blow had left any fangs in its mouth, if it still had a mouth at all—I gingerly picked it up and tossed it a short distance behind me, then wiped trembling hands on my trousers.

"Can we go?" I asked. I wanted nothing more than to see the sun again. And change my pants. I also had some reservations about the advisability of standing about in a tunnel that had mountain lions prowling it.

"I think there's a wildcat or something down here," I added a tad urgently when Cole ignored me. "Maybe two or three."

But he was busy pawing at the wall. It was clay, which I thought was a bit odd, since the rest of the mine's walls had been for the most part rock. And indeed, the seeping water, in concert with Cole's glove, had sloughed away part of the mud to show the rock beneath.

More to himself than to me, Cole muttered, "What the hell?" Without turning around, he thrust his gloved and muddied hand back toward me. He said, "You see a pick anyplace?"

I scanned the ground and spied one under the old shovels. Using my foot to move the shovels aside—and to make sure there weren't any more snakes—I picked it up and handed it to him.

"Good. Now hold this and back up." He handed me his candle.

"All right, but—"

He swung the pick into the wall.

I hadn't been expecting it—the sound, I mean—and I jumped again, right onto the snake. I tripped, fell backward, and went down, all before the clang of it stopped ringing in my ears.

The light went out, too, just like that.

But I hadn't dropped the candle, thank God, and while I fumbled for my matches, Cole just kept swinging that pick.

"How can you do that with no light?" I shouted over the echoing racket. It was the darkest place I'd ever been in. I imagine it was the darkest place anyone had ever been in, outside of the grave.

He was making so much noise that he didn't hear me. I finally found my matches and gratefully lit the candle again. I chanced a quick look behind me, although I was fairly certain that any tunnel-dwelling mountain lions lurking in the shadows would have fled to Mexico by now, holding their ears.

And then the noise stopped. "Took you long enough," Cole said, but his voice had lost its usual growl. Instead, he almost sounded excited. "Gimme that candle."

Carefully, I craned myself to my feet and handed it over. Cole had cast his pick aside, and was kneeling down, looking through the rock he'd loosened. For all that banging, he hadn't loosened very much.

Then he stood up, tucked something into his pocket, and held the candle close to the wall. It looked as if he'd made a little hole, but I could see no more than that. He stood there for a good three minutes, peering and poking, while I rocked from foot to foot, my damp trousers chafing, and then he came out into the main shaft to join me.

"Grab that snake," he said.

It had finally stopped moving. I still held it far from my body, though. "What on earth do you want this filthy thing for?" I asked.

"Told you. Dinner."

I thought surely he must be teasing. Surely he only wanted its skin! He'd make a hatband of it—yes, that was it. Phillip Belvoir, back at Tattinger's, had brought one back to school with him the last term. A gift from his uncle, it had come all the way from New Mexico. It was a handsome thing—certainly handsomer off the snake than on—although Phillip had absolutely no use for it. Clive Barrow had tutored him in Latin for a whole term just so he could see it every now and then.

Perhaps I could convince Cole to give it to me or let me purchase it, and then I could send it to Clive so that he could have one of his own. Perhaps I'd even send him a hat to put it on!

"What?" I asked, alarmed when Cole nudged my arm and rocked me out of my thoughts.

"You gone deaf, boy? Let me take a look at that noggin." He felt the bump I already knew was the size of a hen's egg, shook his head, and asked, "It hurt much?"

"A little." Actually, it felt like there were a dozen

angry dwarves in my skull, all trying to push their way out through the one spot.

"Well," he said, "you'll live, I reckon. Can't see as it's bleedin' much." Then he added, a bit angrily, "Christ! If you'da let that rattler get you, Belle woulda never let me hear the end of it."

I stared at him, mouth agape. If *I'd* let that rattler get me? And he just had to mention Belle, didn't he? An opportunity didn't pass but what he was reminding me that I was inferior: a kid, an Easterner, a person Belle would never be interested in.

Well, in that way.

Perhaps I was from New York, but that didn't make me inferior: things were the other way around, the way I saw it! And maybe I was only sixteen, and Belle might never see me as anything more than a boy, not even when I was all of twenty. But a man— even a boy—has a right to his dreams, doesn't he?

If any of these mental gymnastics showed on my features, Cole didn't appear to notice. He never did. He bent over, snatched my hat up from the floor, and after slapping it sharply across his thigh a few times, handed it over.

"You all right to walk?" he asked.

I nodded. I was a bit dizzy, but didn't mention it. I just wanted to get out of that mine and back into the sunshine again. And as far away from nature as possible.

"How the hell'd you knock yourself out, anyhow?"

he asked as he moved ahead, leading the way up the tunnel.

"Something chased me," I replied, and took a quick look over my shoulder. Nothing but deep shadows, and the faint outlines of endless rock and intermittent timbers. At least our echoing conversation drowned out the tiny squeaks and rustles of the living things in the shadows.

When Cole didn't reply, I added, "I think it was a mountain lion."

He snorted. "No self-respectin' puma'd get caught dead down here, kid. They like to prowl up high. Reckon you got spooked by a bat or somethin'."

Despite the embarrassment of my damp trousers and the throbbing ache in my skull, despite the reference to Belle, and the fact that I was having to consciously put one shaking foot in front of the other just to keep up, I managed to take umbrage at this. "It was not a bat, sir! It screeched at me!"

Cole paused a moment, for we had come to an intersection, then set off again, this time to the left. We were walking steadily uphill, and on top of everything else, my new boots were beginning to bring up blisters.

"Probably an owl, then, Donovan," he said at last, in a patronizing tone. "Never hearda no owls living underground, though."

He was impossible! It was plain that I was never going to win the point—or convince him to stop calling me that wretched name—so I changed the subject. At least he was talking to me. He had probably said more to me in the last ten minutes than in the whole of our acquaintance, not that this was necessarily a good thing.

Scratching my arm, I asked, "Why were you stabbing at that wall?"

He was ahead of me and I couldn't see his face, but I believe his gait faltered, just slightly. "Thought it was funny, that's all," he said. "That rock bein' covered up with clay mud. Guess some fool was tryin' to hold back the water."

"Was that why they stopped that tunnel so short?" I had another scratch at my arm. Something must have bitten me, I thought dismally, because the itch was really beginning to become annoying. "Did they stop because of the water?"

Cole grunted as he trudged on, holding the candle before him. "Likely. If your mine floods, you're sunk. Literally. Pumps cost dear. Sometimes they cost more than the mine's worth. One of the shafts, down a couple levels deeper, is already flooded."

I realized that I was following Cole unquestioningly. I was impossibly turned around and I firmly believe, had I been left to my own devices, that I'd probably be down there to this day. But Cole— despite his many flaws, of which I could have made you a very long list—only faltered twice, and then only for the second it took him to make out our tracks on the floor of the tunnel intersections. We were back up at the surface and crawling out through the boards in less than ten minutes.

By this time, my arm was driving me mad. Before I had walked twenty feet from the mouth of the mine, blinking into the sunlight, Cole grabbed my shoulder. "Let's see your arm, kid," he said with a look of concern.

"Wouldn't you rather go play with your snake?" I snapped, and was surprised at my own crankiness.

"Give it here," he said gruffly. He took the rattler from my grip, dropped it to the ground, and grabbed my elbow.

I gasped. Not because he'd grabbed it, but because I hadn't looked at my own arm until that second. On the inside of my forearm, where the flesh is tender, there was a huge, flattish red welt that itched and throbbed—more so, once I'd had a good look at it. Additionally, the arm felt heavy and achy now, more with each passing moment.

Cole reached toward my face, and I ducked backward.

"What?" he demanded. "I ain't gonna hit you, kid."

"Sorry," I mumbled, and stood still while he held the back of his hand to my pounding forehead.

With a shake of his head, he dropped his hand. "Hot, all right. You feelin' feverish?"

Actually, I was. I nodded.

"Well, you sure been through the wringer today, boy. That's a black widow bite you got, there. Looks like she's took hold, too."

He studied my arm again, poked at a little pit that had formed in the center of that angry welt and was oozing clear fluid. For my part, I never wanted to see the Aztec Princess again. I wanted to tuck my tail and go directly to my nice, quiet whorehouse and crawl into that nightmarish bed and pull the covers over my face until I was twenty-one. Possibly thirty.

Cole let go of my arm. "Ain't surprised," he said. "There was a whole lot of webbin' back where you knocked yourself out. Best change your britches and get settled in while you can."

"While I can?" I nearly shrieked, even as I scratched frantically at my arm. "What do you mean, while I can?"

Visions of Muskrat Hutchins's testicle-biting black widows raced through my mind. He'd said that I'd swell up like an eggplant or a melon or something, and then . . .

I swallowed. "Am I . . . am I going to die?"

Cole bent to retrieve the snake. It appeared quite a bit the worse for wear. At least, it was missing quite a few scales. I knew just how it felt.

As he rose up again, Cole said, "Oh, probably not."

"Probably?"

He looked at me. "You ain't dead yet, are you?"

Numbly, I shook my head.

"Them spiders hit different folks different ways," he said, as if he begrudged the time it took to get the words out. "Some, it don't bother a whit. Some folks swell up and go half-crazy. Every once in a coon's age, somebody dies. But you're still walkin', ain't you?"

In truth, I felt a trifle wobbly in the knees, but I nodded.

"Your head poundin'?"

I nodded again.

"Your arm gone all a-throb? It feel heavy-like?"

It felt like a sack of cement, as a matter of fact, and was thudding to the beat of my heart, stronger and more painfully with each passing moment. All the scratching in the world didn't seem to alleviate either the itch or the ache.

Worse, my thinking processes seemed muddled. For no reason at all, a picture of Clive Barrow popped into my head. He was shaking his fist at me, shouting, "You didn't get me my hatband, you moron! Look at that fine snake. You ruined it! What will the Master of Hounds say, Horace?"

"Sorry, Clive," I muttered.

Thank God Cole didn't hear me. "Well," he said, drawing out the word as he turned on his heel, "you'll probably just go a little crazy."

He headed back toward the horses, the battered snake dangling limply from one hand. His rifle, sending off dull glints in the dying sun, swung lazily in the other. Over his shoulder, he called, "And change them damn britches. I don't wanna smell your piss all night."

7

I suppose things could have been worse. About an hour later the delirium set in full force, but I don't think I was ever completely out of my head. I knew where I was, and that Cole was there through the night, changing the damp cloth on my forehead. And I knew that when my father appeared and lectured me on the proper way in which to eat a lobster, he was no more than a fever dream.

I finally settled into a fitful sleep, and woke midmorning, free of the worst of the fever and its delusions. However, my arm, while improved, was still itchy and swollen and red, and felt as heavy as a lead bar.

"Why didn't you wake me?" I asked Cole as I shakily stumbled to my feet. Besides the weight and itch, my arm still hurt like the devil, too—not a sharp pain, but a pounding ache—and I sat right back down again. I was weaker than I'd imagined.

"Thought I'd let you sleep," he replied. "You were shoutin' and tossin' half the night."

I found this small show of kindness touching until he added, "Hell, you kept me and half the critters in a two-mile radius wide-eyed. You really let somebody named Bartholomew teach you needlework?"

I colored hotly. "I was seven, all right?" Had I talked about every detail of my life?

"Found your cave monster," he said, ignoring me.

"You did? Where?" I sat forward, and was immediately sorry.

"Gone. Bobcat. Good-sized one, too."

A smile of satisfaction had not more than begun to bloom on my face, when he added, "Course, a bitty ol' bobcat's got nothin' on a puma."

I ground my teeth, then asked, "Did you shoot it?"

He scowled. "Why the hell would I do that? It wasn't hurtin' nobody. Came in, looked around, and hightailed it when I threw a rock." He rifled through his pack, pulled out the bag of hard-boiled eggs, and tossed it to me. "I was always kinda fond of bobcats. Better eat somethin'. I finished off the snake."

Tombstone and the Two Bit—and my unmet and colorfully named partner, Mr. Lop Ear Tommy Cleveland—were next on our itinerary, although I would just as soon have given up the entire excursion and ridden north, to Tonto's Wickiup and Hanratty's. The Two Bit was bound to be just as disappointing as had been the Aztec Princess, if that were possible, and I wanted to return to some semblance of civilization.

But I was in no shape to argue with Cole, who insisted we ride southeast to a town called Poco Bueno, where I could see a doctor.

"What could a doctor do that you couldn't?" I asked while Cole helped me mount Tell. Much to my dismay, I was too weak to climb aboard by myself. "Let's just go home."

"What? And put a halt to all this goddamned fun you're havin'?"

And so, sickly swaying in the saddle, I rode to Poco Bueno on the end of Cole's tether line. We arrived just as the sun was setting, and after Cole checked us into the so-called hotel, he set out to look for a doctor.

Now I have said that it was nearly dark when we came into the town, but even I, in my fevered condition, could see that it was little more than a wide spot in the road. And the "hotel" consisted of a one-room shed, roughly ten feet square, owned by a rough and unbathed woman called Mrs. Wiggins.

There were beds, all right, but they had not seen an occupant—or a change of linens—in months. Moonlight peeked between the raw boards of the walls, and when I turned down the lantern, I could actually pick out practically the entire constellation of Orion through one particularly large chink. An hour later, when Cole returned, I was still lying stiffly on top of the covers.

"Where's the doctor?" I asked, and turned up the lamp again.

"Ain't one," he replied. He set a bottle on the wobbly three-legged table. "Why ain't you under the covers?"

"The bugs had a previous reservation," I said snidely. When I'd pulled back the blanket, they'd been as thick as pepper on a pork chop.

"Well, la-dee-dah," he said, and uncorked the bottle. He proceeded to pour some of its contents into the single shot glass he produced from his pocket, then handed it to me. "Drink up."

I eyed it. "Is this some sort of backwoods remedy?"

"Nope," he said. He tilted the bottle to his lips, took a long swallow, then wiped his mouth on the back of his sleeve. "You're about over it, anyhow. The Who Hit John'll help you sleep. And it'll help me get good 'n' plastered."

Just what I needed on top of everything else, I thought as I took a sip. Cole, drunk.

"Don't drink like a sissy, kid. Toss it back."

I did, and immediately fell into a fit of coughing. "If I die," I said hoarsely, once I could speak again at all, "I'm telling Belle on you."

"Be about your speed," he snarled, and raised the bottle again.

I was exhausted and must have dropped off immediately, but I didn't stay asleep long. When I woke it was still dark, and there was no Cole in evidence.

No bottle, either. When I dug out my pocket watch and checked it by the feeble light of the lantern, it said nine thirty.

I sat up on the edge of my cot. I was still feeling a bit woozy, but I had to admit that my arm seemed to be feeling a good bit better. Whether this was a side effect of the whiskey or the result of the passage of time, pure and simple, was a moot point.

I sat there for perhaps ten minutes, bored out of my mind. While I didn't feel energized enough to run a footrace, I was no longer sleepy, and there was nothing to do. I supposed I could take a foot tour of the town. It would only take about five minutes, by my estimation, and would consist primarily of a turn around a hog pen and three or four shacks. How much trouble could befall me? So I splashed some water on my face from the cracked pitcher on the table, put on my hat, and opened the door.

The night was soft and clear and temperate, with a touch of a breeze. About thirty feet across the way, for I could hardly call it a street, was the aforementioned hog pen, with the dozing sows looking far more quaint in the moonlight than they had a right. I supposed the fact that the wind was behind my back had something to do with this.

I set out toward my left down the rutted path, then about a half block later turned left again, toward the light that I had just spied pouring from the open door of the largest structure in town. The building was only about twelve feet by twenty-four or -five, long and narrow and a single story, with a covered porch across its narrow front.

As I neared, I began to make out the crude sign depending from the overhang: JANEWAY'S, it said. WHISKEY AND DRY GOODS. And then I realized that Cole was sitting on the porch, his back against the wall, his arm looped over a nail keg, and the bottle in his hand.

"Hey, kid!" he slurred as I walked up, and lifted the bottle in a wide arc.

There appeared to be only a quarter inch or so of liquid remaining in it. He polished this off posthaste, and tossed the bottle out into the weeds, where I heard it break.

"You got any cash money on you?" he asked hopefully.

"I don't believe you're in need of any more to drink, sir," I said sternly.

"The hell I'm not," he replied, and thumped his head, hard, backward against the wall. I cringed at the sound, although he seemed not to feel it. He only straightened his hat and said, "I'm celebratin'."

I hardly knew what he had to celebrate, unless it was his joy at having seen me humiliated in every possible way, and all in less than seventy-two hours.

I said, "Get up," and held down my good hand. The other one was feeling better, but scarcely had the strength to lever a medium-sized dog up from the ground, let alone a grown man.

Happily, he took it.

Unhappily, he gave it a firm yank and pulled me down to the ground with him.

"Sir!" I sputtered. I crawled off him and tried to regain my feet. "That was completely uncalled for!"

But despite his drunkenness, he was strong, and he pulled me down beside him again. "Janeway!" he bellowed upward, toward the open window. "Another bottle!"

I heard boots on the floor inside, and then a bald head emerged from the window above. "No credit, Jeffries. Why don't you climb on your bangtail and get the hell outta town 'fore the law comes lookin' for you?"

Cole waved an arm. "We don't need your goddamn credit, Janeway. My pal here will pay."

I began to say something, most probably that I certainly wouldn't pay, but Cole threw his arm about my shoulders and took a viselike grip on my spider-bit arm.

"Won't you, kid?" he asked.

"Yes," I said through clenched teeth. "Certainly."

A hand snaked down from the window and dangled in front of my face, fingers snapping. "Two bucks," said Mr. Janeway. "In advance."

Cole released my arm, and I reluctantly placed two silver cartwheels into Janeway's dirt-etched palm. It seemed a terrible waste of cash, but Cole was intent upon it.

"Ain't you gonna ask what I'm celebratin'?" Cole asked as Janeway thumped off.

"You're drunk," I said.

"That I am."

"You're disgusting."

"That, too, kid."

I started to get up again. "I'm going back to—"

He grabbed my shirt and yanked me back down. "Y'know, Donovan," he slurred, "for all them pleases and thank-yous, you're sure a rude little shit."

Mr. Janeway stepped out through the door at that moment, and handed down another bottle of rotgut. While Cole struggled with the cork, Janeway looked at me and said, "If you two are up to trouble, I don't want none of it. Neither does anybody else in Poco Bueno. You see that he gets out of town first thing tomorrow—you hear me, boy?"

I opened my mouth to protest, if nothing else, being tarred with the same brush as Cole, but Janeway disappeared inside before I could organize an argument.

"The nerve!" I said to the closed door.

Cole had the bottle open by then, and proceeded to take a long swig.

"Will you come with me now?" I demanded. I stood up, and this time Cole didn't try to stop me. Through the window, I saw that Mr. Janeway should have been a good deal nicer about taking my two dollars. There was only one man in the establishment, and he appeared to be snoring peacefully, his head on the yard goods. Mr. Janeway, himself, was slouched at the far end of the room, his nose in a seed catalogue.

"Don't get your knickers in a twist, kid," Cole grouched, and slowly levered himself up. This time, I was wiser than to try to help him. I moved to stand well out of his reach. "Where we goin'?" he asked, once he was more or less upright and leaning heavily against the wall.

"To bed," I announced.

"Ain't the same without Belle," he mumbled, and started walking, using my shoulder for a prop.

Gad! He was lucky I helped him at all. Here I was, the next thing to dying, and he had gone out and gotten himself inebriated—and furthermore, brought up Belle again.

As we tripped and wove our way through the brush, I said, "I wish you wouldn't talk about her in that way."

He staggered, and suddenly dragged me a jolting two feet to the right. "She won't marry me, y'know," he said sadly, once he had his balance again. "Asked her twice."

"Good," I said.

"Ain't got no money," he added. "You got money, though, you little skunk. Piles 'n' piles."

"You are delirious, sir," I said. Our rented shack was less than fifty feet away, and I heaved him toward it. "I only have twelve dollars, of which you've spent thirty cents on what laughingly passes for our lodgings, and two dollars more for that rot-gut whiskey."

"Oh, you're a rich little bastard, all right," he said, punctuating the comment with a swing of his sloshing bottle. "Gonna be, gonna be." He took another drink, then stopped stock-still and regarded me fiercely. "You keep away from Belle, understand?"

In the state he was in, it was best not to disagree with him. I nodded, and took the opportunity to scratch at my arm.

"Understand?" he demanded.

"Yes, I understand that you want me to stay away from Belle."

"Damn right."

We started walking again.

"Don't be buyin' her trinkets and doodads," he muttered.

It didn't appear that I'd be able to buy anything for anyone for a long time, considering the disappointment of the Aztec Princess, and that Cole seemed hell-bent on squandering my meager pocket money. "No trinkets," I repeated, and propped him against the side of the shed while I opened the door. "And no doodads."

He fell, rather than walked, in. Feeling that I'd carried him long enough, I simply stepped over him and sat on my bed. My arm was worse again, aching and itching all at the same time, and I had a long satisfying scratch while he crawled the rest of the way inside and sat on the floor, against the side of the other cot. He closed the door with one flick of his boot and tipped the bottle back again.

"Can you keep a secret, Donovan?"

"Why do you insist on calling me that?" I shouted. "It's not my name!"

"So you keep sayin'," he said, a smile curling over his lips. "You know what I got in my pocket, Donovan?"

I threw up my hands, an action I immediately regretted, and rubbed my sore arm, which only got it itching again. "I give up, Cole. Or should I say, Mr. Jeffries."

"Colton Hezekiah Jeffries is the whole of it," he announced almost grandly. "Colton Hezekiah Jeffries, friend to rich men the world over, destined to never have more'n a three cent nickel in his pocket." He toasted me with his bottle.

A nasty smile took hold of my face, I'm afraid. "Colton Hezekiah? It would seem you have nowhere to stand when you make sport of my name, then, sir."

He sniffed. "Don't see me usin' it, do you? And it's gold."

He was off on a new tangent, delirious with drink.

"I would hardly call Colton Hezekiah a golden name," I said with a sigh. I wished I had something to read, and glanced around the little shack. Nothing, not a scrap of newspaper, not even a seed catalogue such as was currently fascinating Mr. Janeway.

"No, you jackass," Cole said as if I were dense. "In my pocket."

"There's gold in your pocket," I repeated flatly, humoring him.

Swearing beneath his breath, he set the bottle down and, with some difficulty, dug into his pants pocket. A moment later, he held his fist toward me. I leaned forward and reached out my hand. He deposited four rock chips in my palm with a soft rattle and clink.

"Told you," he said, grunting as he fell back. "You'd best keep your trap closed about it, too, young Mr. Horace Tate Pemberton Smith."

"You called me by my right name!" I said, surprised.

"Won't last," he said, and immediately passed out.

I didn't look at the rock chips, not until I had poured out the rest of Cole's whiskey (although I took a small drink of the foul stuff myself, thinking it would help me sleep) and gotten him up and onto his narrow bed.

But when all that was accomplished, I scooped the rocks off the table where I'd laid them, and held them in the lamplight.

I gasped.

Gold.

Thin, spidery veins of it ran through the quartz, and fine specks dotted the whole of each rock. I turned the chips over and over, squinting at them again and again, and all the time my insides were knotting with excitement.

They had to be from the Aztec Princess. They had to be the chips that Cole had freed from the wall of that tunnel, and stuck into his pocket, pretty as you please.

And not a word, not a word till now!

I regarded him in the lamplight, and over his snores, I whispered, "Would you have told me if you hadn't been drunk as a lord? Would you have breathed a word, you bastard?"

What could have been his reason for keeping this a secret, other than to cheat me? To think that Cole—a man who, I readily admit, I alternately admired and despised—was low enough to take advantage of a boy! It was almost too shabby a thing to contemplate.

But hadn't he said he was simply a friend to rich men? Hadn't he said he was destined to never have more than a few cents in his pocket?

Still . . .

He was drunk. Who could guess at his true motives?

I stuck the rock chips deep in my pocket and blew out the lamp. Alternately feeling very sorry for myself and rubbing my pocket with excitement, I pondered Cole's reasoning until sleep overtook me.

8

Contrary to my expectations, Cole seemed none the worse for wear when he jostled me awake at dawn. In fact, that morning, and for all the mornings I knew him afterward, he never once manifested the slightest hint of a hangover, no matter how much—or what—he had imbibed the night before.

At any rate, we were moving south before the sun was entirely clear of the horizon, and once again I found myself marveling at the wondrous heavens Mother Nature had hung over the vast desert. It didn't seem to me that they could be made of the same stuff as New York skies, and were probably too magnificent for white men's eyes to behold.

Nonetheless, we were far away from Poco Bueno by the time those intoxicating shades of purple and crimson and orange and pink had faded to the white-hot sky of day, and Cole was still slapping his pockets. It was all I could do to hold back my laughter.

Before we left Poco Bueno, he'd told me to wait outside with the horses, then had gone back into the shed and tossed the furnishings about for a good ten minutes. At one point, the sound of this cot and table slinging—and the tenor of his curses—reached a high enough volume that Ranger spooked a bit. Even my Tell, steady as he was, gave a few nervous hops.

I couldn't have been more pleased.

It served Cole right, I thought, served him right for not telling me about the ore samples the moment he'd found them, for teasing me about Belle and the bobcat and a dozen other things. It served him right for that breakneck race over the desert, too.

Let him sweat a little longer, I thought. If God wasn't inclined to make Cole suffer a hangover, then I could make him suffer this.

Besides, I had never before seen a grown man actually give in to his anger. All the grown-ups I had known back in New York had been of relatively high social standing and good breeding, and were therefore unwilling to show emotions of any extreme, good or bad. It just wasn't done.

Even my teachers had been composed. So to see an adult act mad when he was angry—or conversely, bubble over with laughter, as Belle was apt to do— fascinated me.

But as the day stretched on, I began to feel a tad guilty. Oh, Cole hadn't mentioned the rock chips. In fact, he'd barely spoken at all, although this, in itself, was nothing out of the ordinary. However, by the

time we stopped for the noon meal—jerky and hard-
tack again—Cole unpacked all his belongings and
began to search through them like a man possessed.

I could stand it no longer.

"What are you looking for?" I asked him. It had
fallen to me to water the horses, and Tell was lipping
at the bag I held for him.

"Nothin', damn it," he snapped. He didn't even look
up from his empty saddlebag, which he was currently
holding upside down and shaking fruitlessly.

This display of ill temper nearly put me off reveal-
ing the ore. As I have said, I rather liked it when
people displayed their emotions instead of walling
them off, but I didn't particularly care for it when
that anger was aimed at me.

However, I reminded myself that no matter how
vile Cole's manner was, he'd brought me out here in
the first place, and at my request. I had never so
much as thanked him for that, let alone for nursing
me through my spider bite. If nothing else, my in-
grained sense of common courtesy was off-balance.

I sighed, and said, "Cole?" When he didn't so
much as acknowledge me, I said, a little louder,
"Damn it, Cole!"

This time, he looked up and glared at me.

I dug into my pocket and produced the rock chips.
"Are these what you're looking for?"

He was up in a twinkling and snatched the chips
out of my hand before I could think to prevent him.

"You little turd," he growled, his nose three inches from mine. "You went through my pockets."

I was intimidated, but I stood my ground. "Most certainly not, sir! I have been accused of a few things in my life, but never of being a thief, let alone a pickpocket. You gave them to me last night."

He backed off a foot, and I was grateful since my insides were trembling. Cole was not what one would call overbuilt, but he was a smidgen taller than I and well-muscled, and most likely could have snapped my neck in a trice.

Especially when he was this angry.

But his face softened a little. He tucked the chips deep into his pocket, mumbled something incomprehensible, and turned away.

"I beg your pardon?" I asked.

He knelt down and began stuffing his possessions back inside his saddlebags. Without looking up, he replied, "Said, they're nothin'. Just some rocks, that's all."

"My rocks," I said. I was braver when he wasn't standing next to me. "You said there was gold," I went on, improvising. "You said I'd be rich."

He looked up and stared at me as if I'd just read his private journal. Not that someone like Cole would have kept one.

"I was just wondering when you intended to tell me about it. When you were sober, I mean. And by the way, I was remiss. I should have thanked you

for watching over me the other night. I'm almost
healed, see?"

I pushed back my sleeve a few inches and held
out my arm. Although the arm still suffered somewhat from that odd, aching numbness, the swelling
had almost completely receded. All that was left,
aside from the occasional urge to scratch, was a flat
reddish welt, little bigger than a silver dollar. The
center of it, which had wept and itched so badly
before, was crusted over and healing.

Cole didn't say a word. He continued to stare at
me for a moment, then huffed a short, sharp, half-
puzzled, half-annoyed sigh through parted lips. He
proceeded to wordlessly refill his saddlebags, fasten
them back on the rear of his saddle, snug Ranger's
girth, step up, and gather his reins. From that lofty
perch, he finally said, "Well? You comin'?"

I stood my ground. "When were you going to tell
me?" I repeated. "Never?"

His mouth tightened in what I could only read as
disgust, and he rode out.

It was five minutes before I got Tell ready to travel
and caught him up, and even then he didn't speak
for another ten. At last, he growled, "You think I'd
do that, kid?"

I matched his tone. I said, "I don't know. I don't
really know you, do I, Colton Hezekiah?"

Oddly, a tiny smile crooked the corner of his
mouth. "Told you that, too, did I?"

Honestly, the man was a complete cipher. I didn't say a word.

"Musta been crocked, all right," he added with a shake of his head. "And I didn't say nothin' 'cause I didn't want you to get your hopes up. There's gold, all right, but there's no sayin' how far it goes. Ol' Heck, he was pullin' gold outta that hole along with the silver all along."

I twisted in my saddle. "He was?"

"Don't go settin' off skyrockets. Lots of times they're mixed together. But the silver assayed out at about seventeen hundred bucks a ton. That's raw ore. The gold only assayed out at maybe a hundred and a quarter, a hundred and fifty to the ton."

I tried to visualize how much rock it would take to make a ton. I couldn't imagine that it was very much.

He continued. "Now I don't know how far this pepperin' of gold goes. Could be there's a fortune for the takin' about two feet past where that shaft dead-ends. Could be I chipped out about all there was. Could be that once we start swingin' picks with a little more gusto and set into blastin', that water seepin' through the wall'll turn into a gusher that'll drown the whole damn mine."

"That sample," I said, my voice cracking with barely contained excitement. "That ore sample I found in Uncle Hector's safe. Do you suppose it came from there?"

"Calm down, kid," Cole said, although for once,

he didn't say it unkindly. "I reckon it did. There was a hole already dug into that wall when I started in to pick at it. Looked to me like Heck mudded it up, too, to hide where he'd found it."

I recalled the bush, dead and recently planted, and told Cole about it.

He nodded. "Saw it. Ol' Heck was awful close-mouthed. Didn't even tell me. A feller learns to be that way when he's been nosin' the ground for bright metal as long as Heck."

With some excitement, I said, "But if he knew it was there, if he had a strong suspicion there was gold for the taking—knew it!—why on earth didn't he—"

"Money," Cole said, cutting me off. "Costs a heap of cash to get an operation up and running. Likely he was puttin' a deal together. Heck was sure one for deals."

I slouched in my saddle. I had no money and no contacts. It didn't seem fair that I was inches away from ensuring my future and had no way to get at it. And then I brightened. "Why couldn't we go back there and mine it, just the two of us?" I asked, adding quickly, "I'd certainly pay you a fair share."

Cole snorted out a laugh. "Green as grass, kid, that's you. Sure, we could do it. Until the water comes gushin'. Or some claim jumper puts a coupla slugs in our skulls. Gold makes men loony—don't you think no other way about it. And the whole populace is gonna go plumb peach orchard crazy the second anybody gets a whiff of the first load of ore you bring in. Maybe before.''

I sighed. Each way I turned, he cut me off. ''What do you suggest I do, then? Simply ignore it?''

If he noticed the sarcastic edge to my words, he didn't react. He said, ''Been thinkin' about that. I figure the best thing to do is ride on down to Tombstone and have these assayed there.'' He patted his pocket. ''I figure they'll come in high grade. Maybe as high as twenty-five, twenty-six hundred to the ton. And then you'll take that assay paper, and you'll sell the mine, real quiet and real private. I know a couple fellers who deserve to get rooked,'' he added with a smile that verged on mean. ''Let them monkey around with the floods. Let them blast ten feet back into that rock and find nothin' but more rock.''

It was a two and a half day ride to Tombstone, and all the while I kept thinking about the Aztec Princess, and about Uncle Hector.

I wanted, in the worst way, to ask Cole why he'd had suspicions about Uncle Hector's death, and if he still held them. It had crossed my mind that if Uncle Hector had met with foul play, his discovery of gold in the Aztec Princess might possibly have had something to do with it.

It was a fairly wild supposition, but Cole had said that gold made men go mad, hadn't he? Of course, he'd also added that Uncle Hector was very tight-lipped when it came to things of that nature. It was a puzzle. And every time I came close to admitting that I'd eavesdropped and heard him and Belle in the first place, something happened to put me off it.

I thought over Cole's plan to take advantage of those investors. I wasn't much in favor of it, although I didn't voice my dissent. I figured that there would be plenty of time to do that, once we'd found out what the assay report said, and especially once we got back up to Tonto's Wickiup. There, Belle could intercede on my behalf and hopefully prevent Cole from causing me bodily harm.

I hated to think of myself hiding behind a woman's skirts, scanty though they might be, but not so much as I hated to think what Cole might do to me if he were angry enough.

Of course, if the assay report was disappointing— I still had a few nagging doubts that it wasn't gold at all, that Providence wouldn't possibly be that kind—then we could forget the whole matter. I had no intention of bilking total strangers, no matter what Cole thought.

But if the report was heartening, I had secretly determined to put together a crew of miners and set to the business of bringing out every scrap of ore I could. I was fairly certain I had a foolproof plan for putting together the cash to fund it, too.

As we rode down toward the boomtown of Tombstone, Cole informed me that once upon a time, the place had been known as Goose Flats—a meager collection of shanties and lean-tos on a windswept plain. There had been an itinerant miner there, a man named Ed Schieffelin, who had been told by scoffers that the only thing he'd find in Goose Flats would be his tombstone. He found silver instead, and the little collection of shanties was rechristened.

Tombstone had since boomed into a busy, if rather distasteful, metropolis.

The outskirts of town were an impossibly deep, mazelike hodgepodge of tents and shacks and open-air cooking sites, teeming with all manner and races of people. I saw Chinese, Mexicans, tame Indians, Negroes, and whites mixing and milling about, and more than one fistfight was taking place back in the spaces between the tents. Squawking chickens fled from our path, as did a few squealing shoats and a plethora of cur dogs, and a man was butchering a steer's carcass right on the street.

The place was a whirlwind of stinks and smells. The odors of animal waste and unwashed humans mingled with those of roasting meats and cheap perfume and boiling laundry, and the vaguely sweet undertone that Cole told me was opium smoke. Taken as a whole, it hit you like a fist.

But as we rode deeper into the town, things began to get more organized. The stench faded. The narrow, livestock- and human-clotted lanes between tents became wider and turned into streets. Brand-spanking-new buildings, some looking as if the painters had vacated only moments before, gradually replaced the shanties and tents and open-air ramadas. By the time we ambled into the center of town, there were gaslights dotting the streets

However, this was not to say that Tombstone, even the best part of it, was civilized. Quite the contrary, for it was a hive of questionable activity. Dangerous-looking men crowded the sidewalks and streets, disreputable cowboys and grubby miners and dandied-up gents alike. Half-naked women of all shapes and sizes, even a woman with one arm and another with a thick, dark mustache, hung out of windows and leaned against buildings, hawking their wares. Raucous music and laughter—along with stumbling drunks—spilled from door after door.

If you had taken Hanratty's on its worst night and multiplied it by fifty or sixty, then that would have been Tombstone. And it was only four in the afternoon.

After we settled the horses in a nearby livery and Cole dropped off the ore samples at the assayer's office, we found rooms at a tiny, one-story hotel called Fred's Deluxe. I do not know who Fred was, but I have to say he didn't have very high standards. The wallpaper was peeling, the curtains were in rags, and ancient mouse droppings crunched underfoot. However, there weren't many bugs—probably because of the mice—and the sign said they served lunch and dinner.

Immediately, I sank my weary bones onto one of

the room's two beds. I adored my Tell, but several days on horseback would make anyone long for a perch that had no intention of moving.

Cole, however, tossed his saddlebags and pack on the other thin mattress and announced, "I'm gonna go have a look-see." And then, as an afterthought, he said, "Gimme your gun, kid."

I handed it over straightaway, but gave him a curious look.

"Gonna turn 'em in at the marshal's office," he explained. "They got some kinda damn rule here about not carryin' sidearms inside the town limits."

Just then, we heard a gun's discharge. It couldn't have been more than a block away. I said, "I don't believe everyone knows about that particular rule."

Cole grunted, and tucked my Colt into his belt.

"What about Mr. Cleveland?" I inquired. "And when did the man say he'd have our report finished?"

"I'll ask around for ol' Lop Ear. Ought not to be awful hard to find." His hand was on the latch. "And the feller said tomorrow afternoon. You keep your mouth shut, hear?"

He had warned me against breathing a word of our strike roughly three thousand times while we were en route from Poco Bueno. I breathed a long-suffering sigh and said, "Yes, sir. Who is there for me to tell, for heaven's sake?"

He studied me for a moment, then said, "You'd

best come along so's I can keep an eye on you. Tombstone ain't for kids, Donovan, not even for kids locked up in a hotel room."

I stood up and followed him through the door, saying, "Stop calling me kid. And stop calling me Donovan! My name is Horace."

"I wouldn't let that get around," he said with a smirk as he shut the door behind us. "Especially down here."

Amazingly, Tombstone had a bookstore, and this discovery helped greatly to temper my anger at Cole. While he hiked up the street and checked our pistols with the authorities, I picked out two dime novels. I recognized neither as being members of Clive's collection—and suffered a momentary guilt pang for not having written to him yet—and happily purchased them.

I thought I'd best read up on the West, now that I was living in it, and surprised myself by being excited at the prospect. Well, more the prospect of reading about it than the actuality. I had missed having something to read, and justified the expense by telling myself that I would send them to Clive when I was finished.

With my new books—*Panhandle Slim and the Two-Timers* and *Doc Holiday: Death Comes to Tombstone* (a very popular title, according to the clerk)—tucked firmly in my back pocket, we set out to look for Lop Ear Tommy Cleveland.

Cole inquired at several drinking establishments,

each one of which was more ragged and run-down and scofflaw-filled than the last. At the fifth one, whose staff consisted of a one-legged bartender and three elderly soiled doves leaning on a sawhorse-propped plank inside an open tent, Cole at last got the information he sought.

We hiked for what seemed a mile farther into the rapidly degrading outskirts of town, dodging goats and cockfights and drunkards and beckoning women.

The sun was slowly settling into the horizon and the sky had turned those wondrous colors again, but my stomach was growling and I was impossibly turned around. As I tried to politely dislodge myself from an opiated Chinaman who seemed intent, for some unknown reason, on wanting my boots, I said, "Cole, can't we look tomorrow? I'm tired and I'm hungry, and we're never going to find—"

"Aw, not again!" Cole said, cutting me short, then took off through the crowd at a dead run.

It turned out to be a very good thing that we had arrived when we had, for Cole was sprinting toward a little old ragtag man standing on a wobbly barrel, with his hands tied behind him and a rope knotted around his neck.

9

I knew this was going to be trouble. I shoved my way after Cole, through the mob and toward their intended victim.

The odd thing was, only a couple of them seemed angry. Some were laughing and more than a few were holding beer glasses. On the whole, they appeared more like a group of citizens—granted, the dregs of society, but citizens nonetheless—out to watch an impromptu horse race than to see a man die.

But the two men doing the stringing up were quite serious, and Cole reached the first before I was halfway there. Even over the hum of crowd noise, I heard a pop as his fist connected with flesh. The crowd roared. I couldn't see him very well, though, only glimpses through the shifting crowd, for he had taken the ruffian down to the ground. The poor fellow on the makeshift gallows wobbled precariously on his barrel when the second tough dived after the first.

Excited that their entertainment had been expanded by this new occurrence—a double bill, so to speak—the catcalling crowd moved back to give the battlers more room. I pushed forward through a thicket of elbows and body odor. I reached the small clearing they'd created in the nick of time, for the barrel suddenly spun out from beneath the little man's feet.

I lunged forward and caught him before the rope could pull tight, but the weight of another human, even when it is a small man, is quite a load to unexpectedly come into your arms. I stumbled and nearly went down. Somehow, though, I managed to keep my legs under me, and I quickly shifted my weight and hoisted him up so that his narrow backside was balanced precariously on my shoulder.

The crowd gave another roar—I don't know if it was because one of the combatants had delivered a particularly exciting blow, or that I had saved their intended victim from a premature demise—and the ongoing fistfight on the ground tumbled toward me.

Above, I heard my burden shout out, "Whee!" just before Cole—who was fighting off two big men with no help whatsoever from the throng of onlookers— landed at my feet with an *oof*.

I hopped back, directly into the telegraph pole, and heard the man on my shoulders shout, "Watch it, kid!" and then, "Thick 'em! Thick 'em!"

I had no time—nor inclination—to dwell on this curious remark, for Cole had already regained his feet. I watched, openmouthed, as he landed a blow that broke the first man's nose. It sprayed bright blood over the crowd, and they cheered again.

No sooner had the first man dropped to his knees, wailing and holding his face, than the second man, a rough fellow with a scarred face, closed in and delivered Cole a crippling punch to the kidneys.

Cole grunted, and I squinted in sympathetic pain. He staggered forward and the second ruffian came after him. But Cole wheeled, low and bent over, and rammed him in the belly, headfirst.

Now it was the second man's turn to double over as all the air went out of him. Cole rose up, locked his fists together, and clubbed the thug over the head with them. He, too, went down.

Cole stood there, half-crouched, panting, and eyeing the crowd. "Anybody else?" he wheezed after a moment.

Apparently not a man of them was that big a fool. Also, they seemed to have little stake in the outcome of the execution, other than as an amusement. They slowly moved away and went on with their business, which, by the looks of them, was clubbing babies.

I realized I'd been holding my breath, and filled my lungs again in a rush just as Cole, blood running from a nasty gash above his eye, looked up at the man on my shoulder. He set his mouth in that disgusted expression with which I was rapidly becoming all too familiar, and said, "Jesus Christ! What was it this time?"

"Right good t' thee you, too, Cole," came the cackled, lisped reply.

Cole dusted himself off, raising a cloud in the process, and picked up his hat. He settled it on his head before he took out his pocketknife. I was awfully glad to see that knife. Even with the brace of the telegraph pole at my back, I didn't know how much longer I could bear up under the extra weight.

A moment later, the man on my shoulder was cut free and down on the ground. Well, not really on the ground, because Cole held him, dangling, by his collar. He was a good deal closer to the ground than he had been, though.

"I should've just let 'em croak you, you old buzzard," Cole growled.

"Theems to me like you coulda," the fellow said and inexplicably grinned. He had a wide gap where his front teeth should have been, and all his "s"s came out whistles.

During this, the tough with the broken nose had crawled off, but Scar-face was still there, and was slowly rising to his feet.

"Cole?" I said.

But his back was turned toward the thug, and he was intent on the man in his grasp. "If I'd had time to think about it, I woulda just kept on walkin'," he went on. He lowered the little man to the ground, adding, "You beat everything, Lop Ear—you know that? Why were they tryin' to stretch your neck this time? Poker? Thimble-riggin'?''

By this time, the thug had gained his feet and picked up a length of board. Staggering and weaving, he started forward with an unsteady menace.

''Cole!'' I said more urgently.

But he paid no attention. ''See this piece'a shit, Donovan?'' he said, jabbing his forefinger into the little man's birdlike chest. ''This here's your goddamn business partner!''

The thug was within striking distance. He raised his makeshift weapon, and I did the only thing I could think of. I shoved Cole out of the way.

The board came down and missed Cole by inches, but landed squarely on the grizzled head of Lop Ear Tommy Cleveland. Looking faintly surprised, Lop Ear crumpled to the ground at just about the same time Cole swung around, realized what was happening, and changed his target from me to the ruffian.

Cole's punch flattened the bounder, and across the way, a man standing in a tent opening applauded. The whore on his arm stuck two fingers in her mouth and whistled her admiration. And it suddenly crossed my mind once more that I had absolutely no business being in a place like this.

I didn't have time to think too long, though, because Cole was already picking up Lop Ear. ''Grab an arm, kid,'' he said, and together, we dragged an unconscious Lop Ear Tommy Cleveland out of that warren of miscreants and back toward the center of town.

My business partner in the Two Bit mine revived moments after we reached our rooms at Fred's Deluxe. Which didn't stop Cole from emptying a pitcher of water over his face.

Lop Ear sat up fast, and sputtered, "Why the hell'd you do that?" He shook his head like a dog fresh from the river, and a spray of droplets spattered my face and shirt.

"And why did you have to do it on my bed?" I wailed, wiping my face with my sleeve. My pillow, where Lop Ear's head had rested at the moment of dousing, was soaked.

Cole lit a lamp and turned it up. "Felt like it," he said, shaking out the match. Having dumped out all our water, he snatched my soggy pillow from the bed and, with it, proceeded to wipe the blood from his face.

"Sir!" I said. "That's mine!"

"It's Lop Ear's now," Cole replied with a grumble, and having cleaned the blood off, tossed the sodden, stained pillow to the floor. He peered into the badly silvered mirror above the bureau, touched his cut, and said, "He's bunkin' with us tonight."

I expected Lop Ear to protest, but instead, he broke out into a damp grin and said, "Beholden to you, Cole. Long time since I slept on a piller." Then he turned to me, water still dripping from his face and frayed collar, and said, "Cole's a good boy, even if he's a tad free with that damn water pitcher. Why, he's thaved my bacon more times than—"

"Yeah, yeah," Cole said, cutting him off. Apparently satisfied that he'd stopped the bleeding, he settled his hat back on his head. "Let's go find some grub."

I had a million questions, but my stomach had been growling practically since the moment we'd arrived in town. Hopefully, I said, "The sign said they serve dinner here." At that moment, closest was best.

But Lop Ear shook his head, and a big droplet of water flew off his nose. "I wouldn't eat at Fred's, no, sir. Least, nothin' that you can't tell what it is right off."

Cole appeared to take this under brief consideration. "Aunt Deet's?" he said as he opened the door.

Lop Ear's face lit up, and he levered himself to his feet immediately. "Hell, I can taste that good fried chicken already!" Then he scowled. "You buyin', Cole?"

"Yeah," Cole grunted. "Blow out the lamp, kid." I did, and dumbly followed.

Aunt Deet's turned out to be a café on Allen Street, I believe, and the fried chicken was excellent indeed. Our dinners came complete with country fried potatoes and thick, peppery gravy, green beans with bacon, creamed corn, hot rolls, sweet pickles, and jalapeño peppers. I had never seen nor tasted the latter, and Cole and Lop Ear laughed and carried on when I downed a full glass of water after taking my first—and last—bite.

While we ate, Cole explained my presence to Lop Ear, who seemed genuinely distressed at the news of Uncle Hector's passing. "Goddamn," he repeated over and over, shaking his head. "Goddamn!"

Neither was there good news about the Two Bit. "Drowned," said Lop Ear around a mouthful of mashed potatoes. "She's clean underwater, and even a little baby pump to empty her out's gonna run about a hundred and sixty, seventy thousand. That's U.S. dollars, boy," he added, shooting me a rare glance.

And then he shrugged. "Well, she were about cleaned out when the floodin' commenced. That were thomewhere around five hundred feet or so. Reckon we can just let her drown and say amen." He placed a grubby hand over his heart. "She were a good 'un in her time."

He went back to his potatoes.

During dinner, I had a good opportunity to observe both men, since they were engaged in conversation and paying scant attention to me. Both were eating voraciously—at Aunt Deet's, you could have all the second helpings you wanted at no extra charge—and in this, I joined them.

Both had red checkered napkins tucked into their collars, as had most of the patrons, and both had taken their hats off. This was out of the reverence everyone seemed to have for Aunt Deet, a short, stout, jovial, middle-aged woman who passed from table to table, greeting most everyone by name and asking if everything was to our satisfaction.

It was.

Lop Ear's gray and grizzled hair looked as if it had been cut by a threshing machine gone mad. A variety of lengths, it poked from his head every which way, as if his entire scalp were an unending series of cowlicks. I am tempted to say a good barber could have done wonders for him, but I will not. There was his face to consider, you see.

I don't believe he had been too handsome to begin with, but his nose appeared to have been broken so badly that it lay to, more than protruded from, one side of his face. One cheekbone looked to have been badly broken at some point, too, for his face dented inward on one side where it should have swelled.

The other cheek was striped by three old, long scars, evenly spaced, which ran from just above his eye to nearly his jawline. One of these wounds had caught his eyelid, which, because of the scar tissue, had healed with a distinct droop.

He was not a pretty man.

I couldn't judge his age with any accuracy, but if he was less than sixty, I would have been quite surprised. And I could not for the life of me discern why he had been saddled with a name like Lop Ear. His ears seemed to be the only normal things about him.

After dinner, I wanted nothing more than to go to bed. I hadn't been party to most of the dinner conversation, which had consisted primarily of stories about people I didn't know and didn't care to, or local matters. Besides, Cole had introduced me to Lop Ear as Tate Donovan. Even though I quickly said, "Horace Smith, sir," and held out my hand, Lop Ear apparently thought Cole knew better, and addressed me as Donovan when he addressed me at all.

Loath though I am to admit it, I was becoming resigned to the name.

I yearned for my bed, though. The faster I went to sleep, the faster it would be tomorrow, and the faster we would receive the assayer's report. Also, the faster we would ride north, out of Tombstone.

But the moment we left Aunt Deet's, Cole said, "Let's go get a slug," and took off directly, Lop Ear on his heels. I had little choice but to follow.

Tombstone after dark was frightening, but exciting. Its daytime exuberance had metamorphosed into what I could only call a full-blown, nonstop, rough-edged glamour. The gaslamps on the street glowed bright. Light, both plain and colored by stained glass, poured from every window on the street.

The sounds of enthusiastic music and shouts and laughter had risen by a factor of ten, and the sidewalks were jam-packed with milling bodies. In fact, it was all I could do to keep Cole in sight.

In just a few minutes, however, he disappeared

through an open doorway and into an adobe building. I glanced up at the sign as I elbowed my way after him. THE BIRD CAGE, it said.

This turned out to be a theater as well as a saloon. However, it had nothing on Hanratty's, which, in comparison to this and Janeway's, I was beginning to think of as quite refined. Narrow and oblong and ill-lit, the Bird Cage had more in common with a giant, tinseled coffin than an entertainment establishment.

There was no one on the stage at that moment, but soiled doves were everywhere, including balconies that overhung the area where we stood, and swings that depended from the ceiling. Cole pushed me into a chair just in time to narrowly avoid being kicked in the head by one of these giddy, gamboling damsels.

"Whee!" cried Lop Ear.

Cole signaled for drinks all around.

The noise was deafening and the room was cramped, and more than once I saw someone's coat pull back to expose a firearm. This aggravated me out of all proportion. Why had I been forced to turn in my lovely Colt pistol when everyone else was armed to the teeth?

I leaned toward Cole and shouted, "They all have guns! Someone should summon the marshal!"

He grinned slyly and pulled his vest away from his chest to momentarily expose a small pistol, one I hadn't known he'd owned, protruding from an inside pocket. "There's laws, kid, and then there's laws," he shouted cryptically, then pointed at my untouched glass. "Drink up!"

"And mind your own beeswax, Donovan!" yelled Lop Ear. *Beeswax* came out *beethwaxth*.

I do not know if there was no stage entertainment scheduled for that evening or if we left too early to see it, for by nine thirty both Cole and Lop Ear were almost too drunk to stand up. After some cajoling on my part, they were at last convinced to go back to our hotel.

All the way down the street and around the corner, Lop Ear would stop every fifteen feet or so and, at the top of his lungs, cry, *"Loretta!"*

This wasn't too embarrassing while we were on the main street, since every third man in the crowd was shouting something or other nonsensical. But once we turned onto Fourth Street, which was much quieter, I cringed at every yodel. I didn't know who Loretta was, but it didn't appear that she would be joining us tonight, if ever.

I finally said, "She's coming later, Lop Ear."

Amazingly, this seemed to satisfy him. Drunkenly, he slurred, "You know my Loretta, Donovan? Probably curled up with some goddamn rock breaker." He said something else, too, but just then he walked right into the side of a millinery shop, and I could make out nothing but the "Thumbitch!" that came after.

At last I herded the both of them inside Fred's Deluxe, down the hall, and into our little room. Cole plopped on his cot and made a brief show of elaborately taking off his spurs, but fell asleep—or passed out—before he had the second one all the way off.

Lop Ear simply walked in and fell down.

Unfortunately, he fell directly onto my bed, which left me the floor. I shouldn't have poured my drinks into Cole's glass while he wasn't looking, I thought belatedly. He'd had four or five extra shots that he didn't know about, and I'd had none. If I'd imbibed a whiskey or two, I probably wouldn't have minded so much sleeping on a mattress of mouse droppings.

But there was nothing else for it, and I was so weary that I could scarcely keep my eyes open. By lamplight, I worked a thin blanket out from under Lop Ear and another from under Cole and made a scanty mattress on the floor. Then I blew out the lamp and lay down, head toward the open window on my bloody and still-damp pillow, gave a last scratch to my arm, and fell into blessed sleep.

I was awakened most rudely in the middle of the night. At first, I thought that Lop Ear must have tumbled off his bed and directly onto my chest. Before I could begin to scramble out from beneath it, something big and furry dug its nails into my chest and launched itself onto Lop Ear's cot, squeezing all the air from my body in the process.

Terror gripped me. "Puma!" I tried to shout. "Wolf!" But no sound came out. There was no air to push it.

And then, just as the air whooshed back into my

lungs, I heard Lop Ear joyously slur, "Loretta! You come back," between the sounds of happy little whimpers and a dog's tongue slurping a greeting.

"Lord," I grumbled and, with a grump and a grunt, turned on my side and went back to sleep.

10

The next morning, while Lop Ear lay suffering a hangover, I took Loretta out into the open lot next door and threw a stick for her over and over. She never tired of it. But then, I supposed that when you looked like Loretta you'd take any attention people paid you.

Lop Ear's dog was a match for him, for I had never seen any beast remotely like her. Knee-high at her shoulder and of medium build, she had a coat that couldn't quite decide if it wanted to be short like a Labrador's—which it was, on her face, back, and sides—or long and silky, like a spaniel's. Which it was—or would have been, if all the burrs and snarls and dirt had been brushed from it—on her legs, chest, and thighs, so that she appeared to be wearing a matted bib and pants.

When she was at attention, one ear winged out to

the side and the other stood straight up. Both her lower canine teeth were broken off halfway down, and she had no tail at all, not even a vestige of one. There was no mistaking what she was feeling, though. When she was happy, the entire back half of her body wagged.

These features, taken one at a time, would not have been so awfully odd had it not been for her color. Colors, I should say. First off, there were her eyes: one was a dark brown, marbled through with a soft greenish amber color, and the other was a clear but disconcerting blue. I wondered if she was blind in it.

Her coat was a curious shade of dark, steely blue-gray. Flecked and splashed all through this were patches of black, some quite large, some merely specks. It was as if she'd been black in the first place and some fool had splashed her with a bucket of laundry bleach. The only white on her was the grizzle on her muzzle, and that was not particularly attractive, either.

But she certainly had energy. After an hour and a half of steady toss and fetch, my throwing arm was aching but she was still leaping into the air, anxious for the next fling of the stick.

At last, I could throw no longer. Someone had dumped a battered wooden chair onto the lot, and after I checked it for spiders, I righted it, dusted it off, and sat down. "We will now take a break from our festivities, Loretta," I announced.

She seemed to understand. She lay down in the weeds and crossed her front paws. Quite the lady. I supposed she couldn't help that hideous color.

Actually, I had taken something of a liking to her, the poor thing, but I supposed I'd best not let myself get overfond. Soon we'd be in receipt of the assayer's report, good or bad, and then we'd be off. I teetered between salivating at the thought of all that gold (and all of it mine), and the idea that it would turn out to be pyrite or some such and I'd go back to Hanratty's to live the rest of my life among gamblers and whores.

They were very nice whores, I reminded myself, especially compared to those who populated Tombstone. And Belle . . . ah, Belle. But technically, they were gutter snipes or soiled doves or prostitutes, whatever term you wished to use, and I was unhappy—not to mention morally unsteady—with the thought of riding herd over them.

Not that I couldn't make a go of Hanratty's if I set my mind to it, but . . .

Well, there you were.

"Seen you hurlin' the stick for my Loretta, Donovan. Right nice a' you."

I turned to see Lop Ear walking out toward me. I didn't bother to correct him about my name. We'd be leaving him behind soon enough. Loretta shot to her feet and wagged her matted hindquarters enthusiastically.

One hand shading his eyes against a glaring sun

that, in his current condition, must have seemed four times as bright, he said, "Where'd that Cole take off to?"

I shrugged.

"Like always. Him and Loretta, they got a lot in common."

I raised a brow. "Beg pardon?" At least Cole was reasonably handsome.

"Always runnin' off to somewhere," Lop Ear replied, and scratched the dog's head. She licked his hand in return. "Never tellin' nobody where they's off to. I oughta take that there throwin' stick and give you what for, Loretta."

I was about to protest this course of action when he abruptly squatted down and stuck his face directly in front of the dog, who proceeded to happily lick him from chin to hairline while he cackled.

"That's right, girl. Don't you go forgettin' my ol' ears," he said, turning his head from side to side. It was obvious that his scarred and lopsided face didn't bother her a whit. It was also obvious that she was mad about him.

I simply stared.

A moment later, he stood up again, his whole face shiny with dog spit. "Well, that was refreshin'. You got any cash money, boy?" he asked.

"A little. Why?" If he expected me to buy him a meal, I could afford it, but I had no wish to see this become a habit.

He walked off, beckoning me over his shoulder.

"C'mon, then," he said. "We gotta go take care o' Debby."

"Debby?" I asked as I trotted to catch up with him, Loretta on my heels. For a little man with a powerful hangover, he walked at a clip, I can tell you.

"My mule," he explained. "Vin Tucker's squawkin' about the board. Told me yesterday as how he was gonna turn her into mucilage unless I paid her up-to-date. You got four bucks?"

I had it, although it was over half of my remaining cash. But I supposed that Lop Ear had been my uncle's partner—and was my partner now, albeit in what I now assumed to be a lake roughly ten feet to a side, but five hundred feet deep—and therefore I owed him something. I nodded in the affirmative.

"That's fine, just fine," he said as we turned the corner. "Y'know, you favor your uncle Heck a bit. He were a big gi-raffe of a critter, too, though he were fleshed out a mite better than you. And I do believe you got his jaw."

Rather than take umbrage at that giraffe remark, I changed the subject. "She has rather unusual eyes," I said, pointing at Loretta, and added, "One's blue."

Lop Ear looked at me as if I'd just said, "What ho, there's air to breathe today!"

My face heated slightly, and I quickly added, "I just wondered if she could see out of it properly, that's all."

He stopped and I stopped, too, and he craned his

face up toward mine. "You got blue eyes, don't you?" he said.

"Well, yes," I replied.

"You can see out of 'em proper, can't you? Don't they got no blue-eyed dogs back where you come from?"

We had reached the falling down stable wherein Lop Ear's mule resided, and the moment the balding proprietor, Vin Tucker, laid eyes on Lop Ear, he raised his pitchfork and set loose a string of blistering invectives, which I will not repeat here.

However, after I nervously counted out four dollars and fifteen cents for Debby's back board, he softened a bit. At least, he put his pitchfork down long enough to shoot out a filthy hand and grab the money.

I stood by the open door, just in case Tucker changed his mind about the whole thing, but Lop Ear went back down a row of dim, dank stalls and spent some time with a shadowy beast, who I assumed to be Debby.

"That's just through today, Lop Ear," Vin Tucker called after us with a glower. "Tomorrow she starts addin' up again, and next time I ain't gonna be so dang kind about it!"

Lop Ear turned around, stuck his thumbs into his ears, and stuck out his tongue. Fortunately, Tucker had gone back inside and didn't see. He could have come out again at any second, though, so I grabbed Lop Ear's arm and pulled him around.

He shook himself free and frowned at me. "They manhandle their elders where you come from, too? Must be quite the place." And then he brushed off his grubby sleeve as if my touch had soiled it.

I didn't know whether to be more shocked at what he had done or his attitude about my having stopped him. I couldn't think of a word to say, although I believe I emitted a puzzled huff.

It seemed Lop Ear didn't hold a grudge, however, and soon we were walking back up the street while he commented on passersby. He tipped his hat to one diminutive lady, and after she passed, he said, in a hushed tone that bordered on reverent, "That there was Miss Nellie Cashman, bless her heart. Owns the Russ House over on Tough Nut, raisin' her poor dead sister's five kids single-handed, and the Lord never made no finer angel nor better cook."

And then he tipped his hat just as graciously to a second woman. "Pepper Alice from over at the Purple Garter. Different kind than Miss Nellie, but she'll sure as shit make a man behold his Creator." He followed this up with an exaggerated wink and an elbow in my ribs.

A block later I found myself sitting atop a small barrel in the mouth of an alley. Lop Ear was seated opposite me on a wooden crate so large that his feet dangled. There were quite a few crates and barrels stored there, for the building next door was a mercantile. And while we sat there, Lop Ear had pointed out the sheriff, the man who ran the newspaper, three ladies of the evening, and a luckless miner named Helmut Gehring, who had blown his own leg off with an ill-timed blast, and who hobbled past on a crutch. It seemed he knew every ne'er-do-well in town, either in person or by sight.

"How'd you meet Cole?" I asked. Frankly, I was becoming bored with all the names and faces. I'd be leaving soon, and would have no need to remember any of them, and I trusted I'd never have call to see Tombstone again.

"Cole?" he said, leaning down to give a scratch to the tangle of knots behind Loretta's ears. "Why I knowed him back when he was a pup, round your age. Couldn'ta been more'n fifteen, sixteen."

Strangely enough, the fact that Cole had ever been my age surprised me. I suppose it shouldn't have, but he seemed so completely grown-up and rough and tough that I couldn't begin to imagine him as a mere boy.

"See that ornery-lookin' feller across the way?" Lop Ear asked, changing the subject. He pointed toward a small knot of drunken cowboys who had stopped to harass a Chinaman.

"Which one?" I asked. They all looked reasonably nasty to me. "Shouldn't we do something about that?"

"That tall feller with the black hair and the blue shirt," he said, ignoring my question about the Chinaman entirely. "That there's Apache Tom, and he's a real bad 'un. A for-hire killer. And that feller in the checkered shirt—the one about to throw that rock? That's Johnny Ringo."

He said this as if I should be familiar with the name, but I wasn't. "Johnny Ringo?" I asked. Ringo had put the rock down, and the Chinaman scampered away, down an alley. I breathed a sigh of relief. Not so much for the Chinaman's safety, I admit, but because I wouldn't be called upon to do the right thing.

Lop Ear closed his eyes—not a long journey for that scarred and dropping lid—shook his head sadly, and said, "You don't know nothin', do you, boy? Just keep clear of Ringo, too."

The men moved on down the sidewalk, probably to look for someone else to torment, and I said, "You were telling me about Cole?"

"Oh. Well, your uncle Heck brung him down one time," Lop Ear replied. "That was when I—" Abruptly, he jumped down to his feet, narrowly missing poor Loretta, and waved an arm. "Well, hell and damnation, here comes Cole now!"

Things happened swiftly from then on, because the assayer's report had come in early: over four thousand to the ton! When Cole pulled me aside and whispered the news, I could scarcely contain my excitement. And when Cole then turned around and asked Lop Ear if he'd like to ride north with us for a while, why, I could have throttled him! I wanted nothing more than to be able to jabber at somebody about this great good fortune—even if it had to be Cole—and now it looked as if I wouldn't even be able to do that.

But while Lop Ear collected his mule and Cole went to get provisions and to reclaim our guns from the marshal, I made a stealthy side trip to the telegrapher's office. Cole had said it took a great deal of money to work a mine, and I knew of only one source for that. After all, Uncle Hector had always wired Father, or so Cole claimed. And Father never made a move without consulting Misters Dean and Cummings, his attorneys.

And so I sent a short wire to Mr. Aloysius Dean. I stated no specifics, so as not to inflame the clerk's curiosity more than absolutely necessary. I simply said:

A GREAT FIND! KINDLY EXTEND LOAN TO COMMENCE MINING A. P. SOONEST POSSIBLE. ARRIVING T. W. FOUR DAYS. RESPECTFULLY, HORACE SMITH.

It was a good deal longer than ten words and cost me dear to send, but my excitement was such—and the time so lean—that I couldn't think how to make it any briefer. At least I had the presence of mind to abbreviate both the Aztec Princess and Tonto's Wickiup, which I hoped would throw any Nosey Parkers off the trail. And it never once occurred to me that Mr. Dean might say no.

When I skidded back to the hotel, out of breath and barely able to contain myself now that I was going to be rich, Lop Ear, with Loretta and Debby—who turned out to be a colossal mule of nearly sixteen hands—and Cole and our horses were already waiting for me.

"Where the hell you been?" Cole demanded as he fastened the last pack into place.

"Prob'ly been visitin' one'a them fancy gals I was pointin' out," Lop Ear cackled.

"Sorry," I panted as Cole handed me my pistol. It felt good to have it back, and I paused a moment to run my fingers over the sleek and shiny metal before I tucked it into my holster. "It's almost noon. Couldn't we have lunch at Aunt Deet's before we—"

"You'll eat on the trail and like it," Cole said, and swung up on Ranger.

Cole had proven to me—and all those onlookers back on the outskirts of Tombstone—that he was a ready and able man with his fists. However, he certainly took his time about getting any answers from Lop Ear. We were camped for the night before I found out why those men had been so willing, not to mention eager, to hang him.

We were sitting around the campfire on a vast plain, having eaten a dinner of biscuits, rabbit, and gravy. Loretta was curled at my feet, and I was reading one of my books. It was the Panhandle Slim title, and I didn't believe I had ever seen such wretched prose in my life. Most every sentence in the book was followed by at least three exclamation points, even if it was, "Mary churned the butter!!!" and both the narrative and dialogue were terribly contrived.

I didn't know how Clive Barrow could read such trash. After all, it wasn't as if he'd never been exposed to finer things.

And so I was rather relieved when Cole broached the subject of the impromptu hanging with Lop Ear.

"Aw, them fellers was just bad sports, that's all," Lop Ear lisped. "You'd think they'd appreciate a good-trained trick dog."

"Trick dog?" I put the book down and eyed Loretta suspiciously. She gave her backside a little wiggle.

"See, we goes into a store," he said. "Well, one'a them open tents out there that barters food 'n' such. Don't rightly know if you'd call one of 'em a store. . . ."

Cole shook his head and looked up from the fire, which he was stirring with a stick. Sparks flew up as he groaned, "Tell me you weren't doin' that again, Lop Ear."

Lop Ear just grinned wide, exposing that hole where his front teeth should have been.

I said, "Doing what?"

Cole sat back. "This old buzzard goes in a place and asks for somethin'. A pound of bacon or a short sack of cornmeal or such. And while he's pretendin' to dig into his pockets for his money—of which he never has none—that dog of his comes in, whippet-quick, snatches it off the counter, and runs like hell."

" 'Course," Lop Ear said, "I al'ays pretend to be riled, see? I tell 'em, 'I ain't gonna do no trade here if you can't keep wanderin' curs from mouthin' the merchandise!' I tell 'em their whole inventory likely carries rabies or fleas or somesuch. Oh, I pitch a holy fit, and I pitches it real loud!"

While Lop Ear cackled, Cole said, "Then he catches up with Loretta out of eyeshot and takes the grub. If she hasn't eaten it yet. Goddamn, Lop Ear, it was the same crud in Tucson last fall, when I had to cut you down from the Presidio wall. Hell, you were half choked! You get caught nine times out of every ten. Don't you never learn? Don't you know half the territory knows that damn dog by now?"

Lop Ear grinned wide. "You cut me down, didn't you?" He looked over at me. "Cole here is practical my lord an' savior. He's delivered me from rope and blade that many times, and snatched my butt end from the gapin' mouth of perdition. You picked a good 'un to travel with, young Tate Donovan, you goddamn did. You want to keep your hide on, keep close to ol' Cole."

"Yes, sir," I said. I had no intention of doing anything but that. At least, not until we reached Tonto's Wickiup and Hanratty's, and I was in receipt of a loan from Dean and Cummings.

"You think it over?" Cole asked Lop Ear. " 'Bout the mine, I mean."

I stiffened.

"Reckon I could take a ride out there and have a look-see, maybe do a bit of blastin'," Lop Ear said. "I'd wanna pick up ol' Jingles Beldon, though. There's no better man with dynamite or a flick'a bang juice. You know Jingles, Cole."

Cole opened his mouth, but before he could get a word out, I blurted, "What mine? What mine is he going to blast, Cole?"

Cole's jaw muscles worked a couple of times before he said, "Yours, you little peckerwood. Whose did you think?"

"But you told me not to tell anybody!"

"Settle down, kid," he said sternly. "I told you not to open your mouth, but I never made no such promise. That sample assayed out so rich, I figured we'd best have a gander back into that rock 'fore we go sellin' the whole shebang off to the highest bidder."

While I simmered, he turned to Lop Ear and said, "Course I know him. You introduced us yourself, you ol' buzzard."

Lop Ear smiled. "Just checkin' to see how good you remembered. And you can get down off that high horse, young Tate Donovan. I been breakin' rocks a lot longer than you been alive, and I sure ain't gonna tell nobody about your gold."

Cole rolled his eyes. "Where's he at? And if you tell me he's back in Tombstone, I'm gonna wring your wattled neck."

But Lop Ear waved his hand, which Loretta took

for a signal. She got up and went around the fire to sit beside him. He started to scratch her back as he said, "He's up somewhere around Poco Bueno, I heard. Reckon we could go up there and ask around." Loretta closed her eyes, groaned softly, and leaned into him.

"We just came from there," I said through gritted teeth. It seemed to me that people everywhere were rushing into the knowledge of my gold, people I didn't even know. By the time we actually got back to the Aztec Princess, we'd probably be leading a parade of every hard-luck miner and hanger-on in the territory, all of them set on stealing my fortune.

Well, I didn't want Lop Ear Tommy Cleveland and this Jingles person and Lord knew who else working my mine. I wanted things orderly, businesslike, and with a distinct chain of command. I wanted people with ordinary names like Bill and George and Harold to call me Mr. Smith, or at the very least Horace, if they couldn't bear to be so formal with someone so young as I. And I wanted them to dig so much gold out of the ground that I could eventually go back east, back to Tattinger's, back to New York and civilized people, and never have to think about anything west of the Hudson River, not ever again.

Except possibly Miss Olivia MacKember's Academy for Young Ladies of Good Breeding.

I was absolutely positive that anything in which Lop Ear was involved was bound to end with him dangling at the end of a rope, and me likely strung up beside him. I didn't want to go to Heaven that way, and I particularly didn't wish to meet Mother and Father on those gold-paved streets while wearing dungarees and a Stetson, with a rope around my neck or a big, messy bullet hole through my skull.

"Poco Bueno it is, then," said Cole, and stretched out on his blanket. "There anyplace to roost there besides that shack Mrs. Wiggins has got?"

"Hell," grumbled Lop Ear as he, too, lay down on his blankets. Sighing happily, Loretta burrowed her head into the crook of his arm. "I'd druther sleep under Janeway's saloon than in that bug hole."

11

It took us just as long to ride back up to Poco Bueno as it had to ride down from it, so I was forced to keep uncomfortable company with Cole and Lop Ear for another interminable day. This wasn't to say they were the worst traveling companions—at least, they didn't bludgeon me and leave me for dead at the side of the trail—and Cole's natural stillness was more than made up for by Lop Ear's conviviality.

He was so convivial, in fact, that by the middle of the first day I was ready to speak sternly to him. By the second, I was tempted to simply strangle him. And Cole? Oh, he was silent, silent as the tomb. But on those rare occasions when he did say something of import, it only served to remind me of his betrayal of my trust.

I do not mean to say that everything imparted by Lop Ear was mere babble, only ninety-nine percent of it. When he did have something important to say, it was very important.

I had taken to reading as we rode along through that dusty, cactus-speckled, godforsaken land. My wonderful Tell never spooked and seemed perfectly content to follow the other horses right along, and it made no difference to Lop Ear whether I actively listened or not.

I had given up on the Panhandle Slim book and was reading the Doc Holiday, which proved to be only slightly superior in the writing, but much more exciting. At least, there was no one named Mary in it, and therefore no long, boring, introspective scenes while she churned butter or milked the cow or stood out on the purple-prosed prairie watching interminable sunsets, waiting for Panhandle Slim's return.

I had just come to the part in which Doc Holiday is about to face off with three rough and deadly gentlemen, cattle rustlers by trade, when out of the blue Lop Ear said, "Well, now, I believe you was just a mite, Cole. 'Bout fifteen, wasn't you? That were right after Heck commenced to carry you. I mean, after them damned Apache and all."

Cole grunted, which was his preferred manner of keeping up his end of most any conversation, and I peered over the top of my book. Doc Holiday had experienced some dealings with Apache—fictionally, anyway—in *Death Comes to Tombstone*, and they sounded like very nasty fellows indeed.

"What about Apache?" I asked.

Lop Ear appeared surprised that someone was actually listening to him, and his scarred face fairly twitched with excitement. To let me catch up with him, he reined Debby down to a shamble, which nearly unseated the dog. Loretta rode behind his saddle, and although she braced with all four legs and dug in her nails to keep from sliding off Debby's slick and sloping croup, Debby didn't seem to mind. She was a rather nice mule, if one liked mules. I did.

"Oh, they was terrible," Lop Ear confided, once we were riding head to head. "Them devils, they killed Cole's folks when he was about your age, maybe younger. Course, it were hard to tell with Cole. He didn't get his full, towerin' size until he were practically twenty."

Cole shouted back, "Shut up, Lop Ear," but he didn't turn around.

I was anxious to hear! I dog-earred my page and tucked *Death Comes to Tombstone* in my back pocket. "Where?" I asked. "Why didn't they kill Cole, too? How did it happen?"

"They was headed to California, him and his folks," Lop Ear said, and gestured toward the west rather grandly. "There was several wagons, I'm thinkin'. They stopped 'bout two miles out of Monkey Springs and . . ." He scratched at his ear, then shouted ahead, "It were Monkey Springs, weren't it, Cole?"

Cole, who was riding about fifteen feet ahead, suddenly hauled Ranger to a halt and spun him around. "You talk too much, old man," he snarled, then wheeled Ranger back around and loped out ahead. He didn't slow down to a walk again until he'd put a good hundred yards between us.

As if nothing out of the ordinary had happened, Lop Ear continued. "Yup, I'm pretty sure it were Monkey Springs, 'cause Heck had digs around there back then."

I will admit that I felt a little guilty listening to Lop Ear. It was a bit as if I were going through Cole's bureau drawers, but I hung on every word.

Apparently there were several wagons in the party, and someone had broken a wagon wheel in such a manner that it necessitated a wheelwright. Since they had just passed the little town of Monkey Springs, and since Cole, being smallish, would be no help with blocking up the wagon and wrestling off the wheel, he was sent back to town on horseback. When he returned, leading the wheelwright, the wheelwright's wagon, and a new wheel, there was not one soul left alive.

In grisly detail, Lop Ear described the carnage the Apache had wrought, although—or perhaps because—I cringed. It was horrible for me to hear. I could only imagine what it must have been like for Cole, and by comparison, my experiences with snakes and spiders and bobcats—which I had previously thought horrendous—suddenly seemed trivial.

I shall spare you the specifics, which is a kinder thing than Lop Ear did for me. At any rate, the upshot was that Uncle Hector, hearing about the massacre, had taken young Cole under his wing.

"Right about the time Cole got his height," Lop Ear said, "he took it into his head that he was a fast hand with a gun. Well, he was. So fast it was downright scary, and damned if he couldn't hit what he was aimin' at, too." Lop Ear shook his head, and added, "That's right unusual, I'm here to tell you. But Heck weren't gonna admit it to him. I weren't either, not if I knew what was good for me."

He cackled brightly. "Ol' Heck had him some ideas, he did, 'bout sending Cole back east to school, and he were madder'n a fried toad when Cole took off! Down to Mexico, it was. And damned if he didn't stay gone about four years." He pulled on his ear. "Well, mayhap it were five."

He paused. I was still a bit queasy after hearing—in more detail than anyone needs to know—about the mutilated bodies, and how Cole had thrown himself on his mother's corpse and tried in vain to close her wounds. So I said nothing. There are some pictures you cannot pry out of your head, nomatter how hard or how long you try. It is still a scene that I picture with chilling clarity after all these years, and I was only told about it.

I remember being glad that if my parents had to die, that they had done it far away, in France, and that they had ended their lives quickly in warm, blue

Mediterranean waters. Not at the end of an Apache knife.

Lop Ear paused his narrative long enough to take a drink from his canteen, and the moment he stoppered it again, he said, "Now whilst he were gone, we started hearin' rumors about some gringo gunslinger down in them parts. Didn't have no real name, they just called him El Diablo Dorado. Means "the Golden Devil." Or somethin' like that."

I tried to fix on the name. Anything to shake that bloody picture from my head. It seemed Loretta had heard enough, too, because just then, she jumped down to the ground and raced ahead, toward Cole. Lop Ear watched her go.

"Fickle ol' bitch," he muttered.

"What does this El Diablo Dorado have to do with anything?" I asked.

"Maybe nothin'," Lop Ear replied, switching his attention back to me again. " 'Cept me an' Heck, we thought as how it was kinda funny that after Cole came on back home, we never heard anymore about—" Suddenly scowling, he scanned the horizon. If he'd had ears like a dog's, they would have been pricked to attention.

I heard it, too. "What *is* that racket?" I asked. I noticed that Cole had reined in Ranger, and was staring toward the northeast.

"Whoa up so's I can hear better," said Lop Ear. I did and he did, and a second later a big grin spread over his face. He snatched the hat from his head, and with a sudden and piercing cry of "Whee!" fanned Debby's rump with it. She took off at a fast trot, then broke into a lope.

Tell tossed his head, eager to be after them, but I took hold of him and said, "Easy, son, easy." Cole still hadn't moved from his vantage point, and I didn't think it wise that I did, either.

But a few moments later, a wagon slowly breasted the top of a shallow slope in the distance, and Lop Ear was headed straight for it. Cole eased Ranger into a slow jog, and I followed suit.

As I grew closer, I saw that it was a very curious rig indeed. It appeared to be an ancient short-bed Conestoga wagon, although it was missing its canvas cover. The supports for it were still there, though, and they were strung thickly with what sounded like thousands of small bells of all kinds, all ringing and tinkling and jangling.

But the team that pulled it was odd enough to make the wagon appear almost normal. First of all, there was a ratty-looking sorrel with far and away the worst swayback I had ever seen. You wondered how the poor beast could walk, let alone pull a wagon.

Harnessed next to him was a grumpy, shaggy black-and-white pony. She had a roached mane that stood a good three and a half inches, straight up, and her ears were pinned flat to her neck. I guessed her at barely ten hands high, and the little thing had to work double time to keep up with the sorrel's plod.

The moment the driver reined them to a halt and the bells stopped jangling, the sorrel appeared to lock his knees and doze off. Believe it or not, the pony actually sat down in her harness, sat down just like a dog!

All this happened when I was still a distance from them, and when I got closer, I saw that I had been overkind to call what they wore a harness. It was jury-rigged with more cotton rope and twine than leather, and was strung along every length with more of those bells.

Cole and Lop Ear and the driver were deep in conversation by the time I rode up. I hung back on purpose, stopping a good twenty feet out, staring at those impossible horses and hoping against sinking hope that the creature driving the wagon wasn't the Jingles that Lop Ear had been so keen on having help search for my gold.

He looked a bit taller than Lop Ear but was just as wiry, and had startlingly light blue eyes. They were piercing, even from where I was sitting. He could have been five or even ten years older than Lop Ear, and although his clothing was in better repair he was certainly every bit as much the lunatic.

"That's a right fine horse Heck has left you, Donovan," he called without any preamble, then pointed to the drowsing swayback. "You watch him with my Comanche, you hear? He will savage most any beast what comes near him, and that is a fact. I would surely hate for him to tear up ol' Heck's nice horse."

He took off his floppy hat and held it briefly to his heart, exposing sandy hair shot through with gray, and an odd little bald spot, perfectly round and the size of a silver dollar, just off center on the top of his head.

Then, just as suddenly, he stood up in the driver's seat. Settling his hat back in place, he motioned for Lop Ear to rein Debby out of the way, then hopped down to the ground. "I hear you have got a lot of gold in the ground, Donovan," he said as he went to the back of the wagon and pulled out a long wooden plank. "Me, I have got me a good claim with no bats, but she's goin' to take a lot of blastin', yes, indeed."

As he carried the plank up toward his team for reasons unknown, I shot a puzzled look at Cole. He grinned, just a little, and said, "Kid, this old coot's Jingles Beldon. He's agreed to come have a look at your Aztec Princess."

Jingles had walked to the rear of the wagon again and unloaded a very large rock, and was presently engaged in laboriously carrying it from the back to the front.

"Crazy," I said softly. "They're all crazy." I was totally bewildered. Angry, too—angry that Cole seemed to be hell-bent on telling every madman we passed about my mine. And this Jingles gave every indication of being a madman times two.

As if to drive this point home, Jingles, who I was certain couldn't have heard me, suddenly piped up,

"Ain't crazy, young Donovan. Could a crazy man have caved in practical the whole town of Hanged Dog, and neater'n a pin to boot? I should say not! Did a good job of it for Miss Gini and got paid in gold, but I woulda done it for free, yessir. Woulda done it if I had to pay!"

He dropped his rock a few feet behind the seated pony and made a few adjustments, then picked up his plank. She whipped her head back toward him and clacked her yellow teeth inches from his pants leg.

He ignored this, but plucked a gigantic wad of dirty cotton from her ear and shouted, "Will you take your feet, you midgety she-devil?"

As if all this were perfectly normal, Cole backed Ranger out of the way, and Lop Ear backed off a few more feet, too. Loretta, who had been standing several yards off to the side, ran behind a clump of brush and peeked out around it. As the sorrel, Comanche, commenced to snore rhythmically, the pony swung her head back and forth, ears still pinned flat.

"So much for you, then, Grace," said Jingles, and reinserted the cotton.

The pony yawned in reply.

I watched, gape-mouthed, as he picked up the board, worked one end of it between her rump and the ground, then turned it so that the middle of it was sitting on that rock, like a child's seesaw.

Without warning, he leapt straight up, onto the high end of the board, and just like that he levered that pony up onto her feet. Well, I don't know that he actually levered her, because it seemed to me that the pony stood up a fraction of a second before he landed. But still, it was an amazing piece of business. I had never seen anything quite like it.

"Whee!" cried Lop Ear, and smacked his thigh.

Cole just sat there.

Jingles lugged the rock back and settled it in his wagon bed, then tossed the plank in after it and climbed back up to the driver's seat. "Well, I'll be seein' you, then," he called, and picked up his reins.

I believe I gave an audible sigh of relief. It seemed that he had forgotten all about my gold, and was going home. But before he had time to snap the reins over the team's rumps, Lop Ear said, "What about the Aztec Princess?"

I could have murdered him.

Jingles paused. "Got to get my supplies back to camp first. Everything in its order. Got me some bang juice and bottles, lots of bottles, and a smidge of flour and grease and feed and the like. Had to order the bang juice special, clear from Tucson. Can't get it around here, no, sir. Bunch of dang dirt farmers and low women and robbers in Poco Bueno. That Janeway will steal a man blind."

Cole thumbed back his hat. "You tellin' me you're hauling a load of nitro around in that thing?" He pointed at the wagon.

"Not exactly, not exactly," allowed Jingles. "But if she sits around long enough, she'll commence to sweat like a Texican well digger. Course, I used to fling it at my bats, but . . ." He shrugged.

Cole nodded as though he knew what the devil Jingles was talking about. "How much you got?"

Jingles screwed his face up. "Ten cases," he said, then confided, "I like to be prepared for the worst."

Lop Ear locked his hands on Debby's saddle horn and leaned back. "Ten cases?" he cackled. "Hell, you just like the blastin' better than the findin', Jingles."

"Like you're one to talk, you old rake-faced coot!" Jingles snapped.

"Scalp head!" Lop Ear rejoined, and stood up in his stirrups.

But before the squabble could turn into a full-blown fight, Cole said, "Whoa, whoa, whoa, you two! How 'bout I buy those bang sticks off you, Jingles? Save us time and nosy clerks. I'm especially wantin' to avoid nosy clerks, if you take my meaning."

Jingles squinted and scratched the back of his neck for a moment. "That'd do, I reckon," he said at last, much to my disappointment. "Well, let's be off to the Aztec Princess, then. Still in the same place, ain't she?" He slapped his reins over the team and hollered, "Git up!"

The bells started jangling as Comanche started sleepily plodding again and the pony Grace trotted to keep up. Cole, riding beside the wagon, had to shout over the racket for about five minutes to convince Jingles that since it was almost four o'clock and

Poco Bueno was a scant three miles away, we'd best spend the night there.

I think what finally convinced him was that Cole offered to buy the drinks.

Which, of course, meant that I would.

An hour later, we had entered Poco Bueno and settled the horses into Mrs. Wiggins's makeshift corral. While Tell and Ranger and Debby went straight to work on the hay we pitched them, little Gracie went directly to the far end of the enclosure and sat down. No one so much as commented on this, and in fact, Jingles carried some hay down to her.

He also insisted that Comanche be staked out, away from the other horses, since he feared the gelding would do them damage. Had anyone asked me I would have said a half-starved jackrabbit with enough incentive could have killed that horse, or at least crippled him for life. But as no one asked, I kept my own counsel.

At the insistence of Cole and Lop Ear, we walked over to Janeway's, kicking the tumbleweeds from our path as we went.

"Don't know how they got the nerve to call this a town," Lop Ear commented.

"Well, they have sure as shootin' got them a sheriff," Jingles said. He pointed down the street, which was vacant as far as the eye could see, save for four or five widely spaced buildings with multiple weedy lots between them. Someone had dreamed big dreams for Poco Bueno, but they hadn't come to fruition.

"That overgrown outhouse is where Biggs hangs his badge," Jingles continued, pointing to the smallest structure. "I don't believe you could get a full-grown cow in there, not horns and all. And for sure not a longhorn, like they have over in Texas. Why, some o' them got horns that spread eight, ten feet! Cole, I ever tell you about the time I rode me an elephant?"

Mercifully, we had arrived at Janeway's, and Jingles's story was cut short.

"You again?" Janeway growled when we walked in. I did not believe Mr. Janeway had much chance of success if he treated all his customers in such a fashion, but I kept my mouth closed. It was getting to be a habit.

"Not thrilled about it myself," Cole replied, then nodded at me.

I plunked two silver cartwheels on the splintery counter.

"Bottle of whiskey," he said.

Grumbling, Janeway fetched it and the glasses, and the four of us found places to perch amid the calico bolts and nail kegs and flour and sugar bins. Cole poured the whiskey.

There was one other customer in the place. A large man—not quite so tall as Cole, but certainly bigger in girth and vastly more repugnant in expression— stood at the small bar in the rear of the store, sipping a beer. I decided that he was passing through, also, as he had a good bit of desert dust on his clothing and boots. And also because his horse—anyway, I assumed it was his horse—was tied out in front of Janeway's. He nodded at Cole, who nodded back. It wasn't a nod of recognition, simply one of acknowledgment.

Cole and Jingles and Lop Ear started up what they must have thought was a cleverly deceptive conversation about the various catastrophes that could strike cattle. Mercifully, they didn't seem to expect me to participate. One could only take so much of hearing about blowflies and hollow tail and scours and such, and when Cole wasn't looking, I poured the last of my drink into his glass. I had tasted it, and found it as vile as the last time. Then I stood and carried my glass to the bar, in order to keep someone from filling it again.

Just as I set it down next to a gigantic jar of green and slimy-looking pickled eggs, Janeway wiped his beefy hands on a filthy bar towel and announced, "I'm goin' to the shitter. Anything's gone when I get back, Jeffries, I'm gonna know who took it." He sent Cole a nasty look.

Cole snorted and went back to his conversation.

Now, since we had come into Janeway's, the rough-looking man at the bar had been watching me. I don't mean to say he was blatant about it, but every time I looked around I got the feeling that he had just taken his eyes away from the back of my neck.

And as Janeway went out the door, the big man said, "Hey, kid. You from around here?"

I was torn between being a little afraid of the brute, and being pleased that he'd noticed my manner was vastly more civilized than my companions'. I took the middle road. I said, "You have guessed correctly, sir. I am a native of New York City."

The conversation behind me trailed off into nothing.

The big man smiled, although there was nothing friendly in it. "That right?" he said. "And what would you be called?"

Automatically, I replied, "Horace Tate Pemberton Smith, sir. And you?" Manners are a hard thing to let go when one has been drilled in them, and automatically, I stuck out my hand.

What happened next came so fast that it is difficult to put it all together, but I will try.

Instead of taking my hand and shaking it like a gentleman, the man let his unfriendly grin broaden into something wholly evil. Low, he said, "Well, ain't this my lucky day?"

Like lightning, he drew his gun.

Before I could think what to do, he fired. Except that I heard two shots, not one, and I wasn't dead. At least, I didn't think so. My knees turned to aspic and I grabbed the bar to keep from crumpling to the floor. I remember catching a glimpse of Jingles as he wrested my Colt from its holster and shoved Cole's still-smoking pistol into my numb hand, even as the brute collapsed face-first into the yard goods.

I remember Cole growling, "See? What'd I tell you about that Horace shit? And why'd you give him my goddamn gun, Jingles?"

A rolling bolt of calico came to a stop against my boot just as Janeway, trying to rebuckle his belt and run at the same time, came barreling back through the door, followed directly by a medium-sized man with a bent tin badge pinned to his chest. The man with the badge was shouting, "What! What!" And then he saw the body.

Janeway had taken it in, too. He bellowed, "Cole Jeffries! I knowed it! I just knowed it!" With both hands balled into hamlike fists, he went past me toward Cole, hopping bolts of cloth and crates of supplies the falling body had scattered.

I hadn't the presence of mind to turn around, but a second later I heard a loud thump and a wet crash, and Janeway stopped yelling. Dozens of pickled eggs rolled out across the floor, spraying brine and strong pickling smells over boards and boots.

The sheriff was kneeling beside the body by this time. "Goddamn," he said, ignoring Janeway's plight entirely. "Deader'n my wife's iron." And then he looked up at the gun held limply in my hand, and at me.

I have no idea what was on my face at that time.

I was incapable of speech or rational thought, and my boots were rooted to the floor. In my defense, I had never had a man drop dead in front of me before, and with absolutely no warning. I probably would have soiled my trousers again if I'd had time to think about it.

Lop Ear stepped forward into my range of vision, carefully avoiding the eggs. "I theen the whole thing," he lisped, pounding his chest. "It were thelf-defense."

"That's the truth, Sheriff Biggs," Jingles chimed in from behind me, as serious as a bishop on Sunday. "This big wad of nothin' drew on the boy, and for no reason a churchgoin' man like yours truly could figure. Now one time when I was up Colorado way—"

"Shut up, Jingles." Cole, looking well past annoyed, stepped forward, kicking eggs and brine-spattered yard goods out of his way. "Just close your pieholes, both o' you. What happened was—"

But the sheriff, who had rolled the body over on its back, cut him off. He let out a long whistle and said, "Well, paddle my ass and call me Dorey! You yahoos know who this sombitch is?"

My companions shook their heads in unison. I was still too stunned to do anything.

Smiling ear to ear, Biggs picked up an egg, wiped it on his shirt, and took a thoughtful bite. Chewing, he said, "This here's none other than John Henry Strider hisself!"

12

The name meant nothing to me, but someone—I think it was Jingles—suddenly hissed in air. I heard Cole murmur, "Aw, shit!" He sank down on a pile of crates and wiped his face with the flats of both hands.

"You done the shootin', did you, boy?" the sheriff asked me.

I moved my mouth, but nothing came out. Images flashed through my mind, images of being marched to the gallows, of being hanged, of my body left to rot as a warning to others, and of my entire class from Tattinger's being shipped across country to view it.

Sheriff Biggs's eyes flicked to Jingles. "What's his name?" he asked, still chewing.

"Donovan," Jingles piped up far too gleefully.

"Tate Donovan," added Lop Ear.

"More often called Kid Donovan," Jingles corrected, and stepped on Lop Ear's foot by way of punctuation. "Oh, he's a good hand with a gun, 'specially for a fella so short in years. Why, the mind boggles, thinkin' how fast he'll be once he hits his majority." He elbowed Lop Ear in the ribs. "Killed himself John Henry Strider! My, my. Chalk up another one for you, Kid."

Softly, Lop Ear growled, "Stop pokin' at me, you consarned scalp head." He took a step away.

"Claw-faced old coot," Jingles happily muttered back. "Oh, young Donovan is fast with a gun, Sheriff Biggs. He has got the population of Tombstone what is dastardly—that's more'n three quarters, by my reckonin'—fearin' to go out in the daytime lest they incur the might of his saintly wrath. Why, he is a terrifyin' messenger of good, and a defender of kids, and—"

"Shut up, goddamn it!" shouted Cole—a little too late, by my book—and he was so angry that veins stood out in his forehead. Behind us, Janeway twitched and moaned, and a new shower of those smelly pickled eggs came bouncing out across the floor, spraying juice and picking up dirt.

Hands clenched into tight fists, Cole rose from his perch. Visibly struggling to keep himself under control, he said, "It wasn't like that, Biggs, and these two old desert rats damn well know it. I was the one that did the shootin'. And then this mule's pizzle," he said, jabbing a finger toward Jingles, "he grabbed my gun and switched it with the kid's."

Biggs got up from the floor and dusted his knees. "Just like you to try an' swipe the credit, Jeffries," he grumbled with a disgusted shake of his head. "Well, I'm here to tell you that I ain't buyin' it for a slap second, no, sir. Why, I practically seen Kid Donovan shoot him my own self. Ain't he still holdin' the gun?"

"That's right, Biggs," Jingles chimed in. "Amen and pass the gravy!"

Cole thundered, "But it's my gun!"

Biggs closed his eyes and wagged his head. "No buts about it, Jeffries. There's a gun already stuck in your holster, so shut your face and save your lies for those that'll believe 'em."

Biggs turned back toward me. "Sorry to say there ain't no bounty on John Henry here," he confided apologetically. "He al'ays managed to pull off his killin's legal-like, rat bastard that he was. He was up to thirty-seven, the last I heared."

Jingles scratched his head. "Forty-one, I was told. Course, I heard he was in New Mexico, too. Hired himself out to Mammoth Mines, they said. It's a big operation, Mammoth," he added. "Lots of silver, lots of skulduggery."

Lop Ear snorted derisively.

A hatchet-faced man, painfully thin and dressed in patched overalls and a sagging hat, peeked around the doorway and surveyed the scene. "E-everythin' all right, Biggs?" he asked nervously. "Me and Electa heard a couple shots."

"Will you listen to me, Biggs?" Cole tried again. "This idiot kid didn't—"

"I told you to shut the hell up, Jeffries," Biggs half shouted. "You think I'd take the word of some lyin', thievin', no-'count, go-to-Mexico, gunslingin' sonof-abitch over Jingles? He might be half cracked, but he don't lie."

Jingles rocked back on his heels and slid Cole a smirk. Cole angrily raised a threatening hand, but Lop Ear, who was standing between them, put a stop to it.

"And would you mind holsterin' that pistol, Kid?" Biggs continued. "You're makin' me nervous." He turned around to face the door. "It's all right, Carl. Kid Donovan just shot hisself John Henry Strider!"

"John Henry Strider?" Hatchet-faced Carl gasped and took off down the street as if the devil himself were on his tail, shouting, "Kid Donovan shot John Henry Strider at Janeway's!"

"Now you listen to me," Cole began, and took a step forward.

"How many times I gotta tell you to shut the hell up!" shouted Biggs.

Somehow, I managed to slide Cole's Colt into my holster, and at last I found my voice, or the beginnings of it. I put one hand on Cole's chest in an attempt to hold him back, and said, "Sh-Sheriff Biggs, sir, this gentleman drew his pistol with no warning. Cole was only attempting to . . . Sheriff?"

Biggs wasn't listening, for he had dropped to his

knees again. My first thought was that he was diving for another of those putrid eggs, but he put his hand on my boot. "Holy shit," he muttered. "Will ya take a look at that?"

I had not moved my feet a fraction of an inch since I first offered my hand to the dead man, but now I looked down to where Biggs was pointing. The late John Henry Strider's bullet had entered the floor right next to my foot, leaving a round and splintered hole. It had also taken a small, crescent-shaped bite out of the edge of my boot's sole.

"I'll be damned," said Biggs, and levered himself up again. "I'll just be dinky-double damned. Kid, I'd like to shake your hand."

Not knowing what else to do, I numbly stuck my hand out and he grasped it firmly. "Steel," he said, pumping it over and over, "that's what you are, Kid, pure steel. I'm right sorry I ain't never heard of you before, but we're kinda the armpit of the prairie out here in Poco Bueno. Don't get much news. Kid Donovan in my town, by God! Faced off with John Henry Strider point-blank and didn't flinch!"

We vacated Poco Bueno immediately, at the suggestion of Sheriff Biggs. He was worried that I'd take down Mr. Janeway, too, once he woke up. He confided to us that Mr. Janeway was a bullheaded bastard, but he was the bullheaded bastard who owned Poco Bueno's only store, and therefore he'd rather not bury him.

"I trust you see my meanin', Kid," he'd said. "No offense."

He was most solicitous. I'll give him that. He didn't even object when Lop Ear, whose shirt bulged as if he had gained ten pounds since we had entered Janeway's, started calling, "Loretta! Loretta! Where you got to, dagnab it!" at the top of his lungs.

"No offense taken, Sheriff," I replied. I'd gotten over the worst of my paralysis and confusion while Biggs—along with a fawning Carl and most of the citizenry of Poco Bueno, which amounted to about two dozen people—trailed after as we marched down to the corral. However, I hadn't had a single second out of Biggs's earshot to confer with any of my companions.

Although I was heartily tempted to try, once again, to press the truth upon Biggs, I was also leery of it. This John Henry Strider person had died, after all, and had died by violence. Even though he might have been a bad man—and I had every indication that he was—someone needed to shoulder the blame. Preferably the perpetrator.

But Sheriff Biggs seemed to already know Cole far too well, and bore a dislike for him so strong that he wouldn't listen to a word Cole tried to say. The basis for this enmity was unknown to me, and I thought that I'd best ferret out the reason before I started pointing any fingers in Cole's direction.

At least Biggs—and in fact, all of Poco Bueno—seemed delighted over John Henry Strider's untimely and violent demise. It seemed an odd position for an officer of the law to take, but all things considered, I was not about to argue.

Besides, with a depth of gratitude I could not fathom, Mrs. Wiggins tearily refunded the money we had paid for the use of her corral and one night's rental of her shack. Men took off their hats to us, and a couple of them shyly shook my hand. A little boy pointed at me and asked, in a rather loud voice, "Is he the one, Daddy?"

And all the while we were tacking up the horses in preparation to vacate the town, and children perched on the fence and grown-ups whispered and doffed their hats, Lop Ear and Jingles chortled softly and Cole grumbled under his breath.

The sun was still hovering above the horizon as we rode north to the clatter of Jingles's bells, out of Poco Bueno. The tardy Loretta caught us up and leapt behind Lop Ear's saddle just as we passed the final shack and noisily headed out into open desert again, dodging stray tumbleweeds.

Two hours later it was dark, and we were camped well away from that paltry excuse for a town. I had kept to myself since we left town, distanced at first by the awful racket of those bells, and later by purposely offering to see to the horses, single-handed. I couldn't help but overhear Cole and those two old goats, though, and I was getting awfully sick of it.

The smells of good cooking rose to meet me as I

finally and reluctantly joined the others at the fire, and as I sat down, Cole was saying, for at least the thousandth time, "I shoulda just shot you, Jingles."

I was almost hoping he would make good his threat. There would be one less crackpot fiddling with my gold, and one less person carping around the campfire tonight. All I wanted was some silence in which to sort it out.

At the end of my figurative rope, I asked, "Why don't you do it, then, Cole? Go ahead. Just shoot him. If you get it out of your system, will you be quiet?"

Cole set his mouth and glared at me over the fire. Lop Ear, having suddenly lost his extra weight, had the coffee going and a skillet of biscuits baking. Another sizzled with the fragrant ham that I had smelled all the way down at the picket line, and that I was reasonably certain he'd stolen from Janeway's store. Compared to everything else that had happened in the past few hours, the theft didn't seem worthy of comment.

"After all," I added stubbornly, "one man has already died at your hands today. What's another?"

Lop Ear chortled and reached around Loretta to crack stolen eggs in with the ham.

Jingles made a sour face. "Now what kind of an attitude is that to be takin'?" he asked, and theatrically slapped a liver-spotted hand over his heart. "I have saved your bacon today, young Donovan, not to mention Cole's. I have taken a sorry situation and turned it around into a tale of masterful glory and gunslingin' to tell round the fire. And now you're incitin' him to massacre me." Jingles shook his head sadly. "Why, I have not been subjected to such unfair treatment since Dewey Hoofman tried to throttle me in my sleep for being a hog thief. Never thieved so much as a shoat in my life! I have took a few chickens and a cow or two, mind, but never a hog, and Dewey never kept no chickens."

Fiercely, Cole jabbed at the fire with a stick. There was a light wind, and Lop Ear had to scurry to the side to avoid the sudden shower of sparks that billowed his way. Loretta didn't move as fast, however, being preoccupied with an eggshell. Over the faint stench of singed dog hair, Cole demanded, "And just how do you figure that, old man?"

Jingles's brows shot up. "Why, Dewey never had so much as a feather on his place! Couldn't abide a bird, not after the vultures polished off his poor daddy's molderin' corpse down in—"

"Hold it," Cole said with a wave of his stick. "I mean, how you figure you saved anybody's bacon?"

Jingles pursed his lips. "I suppose you have forgot how you crossed Janeway's brother-in-law up in Flag that time, or—"

"He deserved crossin'," Cole cut in.

"And he was still a man's brother-in-law," Jingles said, lifting his nose into the air. "Mayhem and rowdy-dow don't count diddly when it's a man's kin that's accused of them, even kin by marriage. And the ones with the god-awfullest, scum-suckingest kin is the most defensive." He shook his head. "As for Sheriff Biggs, I don't know why he has it in for you. But he surely does, and by doubles."

He brightened a little, and added, "Now this reminds me of the time I was down around El Camino, and these two brothers . . . I believe Nate and Dave Blanchard was their names . . . Well, old Dave had a purple birthmark over near half his face, and they had an old red cowdog named Susie with 'em. Anyhow, they showed up in my camp madder'n a couple of boxed bobcats on account of they thought I'd made off with their camel. . . ."

"Mayhap it were in them years when you was down to Mexico, Cole," Lop Ear cut in happily. "When you was down there, did you shoot Biggs's brother, too?"

Cole glared at him.

"Why," said Jingles, miraculously back on the subject again, "if I hadn't switched that pistol of yours, you'd be danglin' by your neck from Janeway's porch right this minute. A man can die a lot of places, Cole, but Janeway's front stoop is not one I'd pick."

Cole grumbled something I couldn't make out, and then he tossed his stick into the fire. He looked at me, ignoring Jingles completely. "I should have stopped it, kid. I'm sorry. Shoulda put the kibosh on the whole damned thing."

I softened a little. Hearing Cole actually say he was sorry about something—about anything—was what did it, I suppose. I said, "Well, everything was so confusing. I should have said something myself, except that I was—"

"Pure dumbfounded, boy!" cackled Lop Ear, and he slapped his thigh. "Never seen another white man so thunderstruck in all my borned days!"

"I suppose I was," I admitted, and smiled a bit sheepishly.

"You're takin' this way too light, kid," Cole said. He leaned forward. "Don't you know about John Henry Strider?"

"He was someone who killed a lot of people?" I ventured. It was the sum and total of my knowledge of the man.

"Damn right," replied Cole. "He was a hired gun. Worked for the mining interests, or anybody who'd hire him. And he had a reputation."

Serious for once, Jingles nodded.

Lop Ear, turning the ham, muttered, "That he did, that he did."

"A reputation for what?" I asked.

Cole let out a quick little huff of air. "For bein' fast, you idiot. For bein' deadly. I'm tellin' you, I should have stopped it—somebody should have—because once word gets out that you killed that shootist, you're gonna have every quick-draw Johnny in the territory on your tail."

I'm ashamed to admit it, but I honestly did not understand him. "Whatever for?"

"Tryin' to kill you, that's what!" Cole roared, and

swept his arms wide. "This ain't New York! This ain't even Missouri, goddamn it! Out here, bein' fast with a gun's the only claim to fame some men have got. And if gunnin' you down is a way to make that claim bigger, they're gonna come after you. Make no mistake."

Belatedly, the gravity of the situation settled over me. Men, coming after me? I had yet to fire my pistol, and I couldn't imagine aiming it at another human, not even to save my life. I hunched over my knees, hugging them. "Dear," I muttered. "Oh, dear!"

"Oh, dear," parroted Lop Ear. "Goodneth grathious!"

Jingles rubbed at his nose. "Well now, I reckon I didn't think about that, Cole. A feller can't be perspicacious every dadgum second of the day, you know. Young Donovan, I hereby humbly apologize for any grief that may come to you."

"Please!" I said, wearily closing my eyes and fervently wishing that my parents had never gone to France, that they'd never been killed, and that I was back at school, innocently studying Latin and mathematics and feeling sad for myself because my allowance was late in coming. "My name isn't Donovan. For the millionth time, it's Smith!"

"First time I heard of it," remarked Jingles, and stared out into the darkness. "You tether my Comanche far enough from those other horses?"

"Whatever your name is, what's done is done," pronounced Lop Ear. "And so's these biscuits."

13

It took us nearly a full day to ride from our camp outside Poco Bueno to the Aztec Princess, mostly because the wagon slowed our progress over the increasingly rugged terrain. While Jingles's wagon rattled and banged and bumped over dusty ruts—or worse, virgin desert—the noise of those damnable bells kept our conversation to a minimum. This was fine with me, as I had a great deal to mull over.

John Henry Strider, for one. Why on earth had he asked my name? This had only flickered back into my memory somewhat after the fact, and it struck me as very curious. And what had he said when I'd told him? "Ain't this lucky," or some such. Why, it was as if he were looking for me!

I tried to banish this impossible notion from my mind. Perhaps Cole had been right after all. Perhaps hearing the name Horace simply brought out the worst in Westerners.

And, all things considered, I supposed I could forgive Jingles for snatching the pistol from my holster and filling my hand with Cole's gun. After all, now that I'd heard about the bad blood between Janeway and Cole—and, more mysteriously, between Biggs and Cole—switching pistols must have seemed, to Jingles's twisted logic, his only recourse.

I wished it had occurred to him to stick the firearm into Lop Ear's hand instead of mine, though.

Additionally, I had a case of nerves about the telegram. I thought that perhaps I should have given Mr. Aloysius Dean a firm figure for commencing operations on the mine, but then, I hadn't the slightest idea what that might be. Not without consulting Cole, anyway.

But then, I reasoned, hadn't attorneys Dean and Cummings—on father's behalf—done this sort of thing for Uncle Hector many times before? They, above all others, should be able to ascertain the proper funding. With any luck, the money should be waiting for me when we got back to Tonto's Wickiup. If we ever did. Our progress was so slow, what with having to clear brush every few minutes so the wagon could get through—and Jingles having to "lever up" his pony every other time she stopped— I was beginning to wonder.

Each time we paused to rest the horses and that damnable din of bells stopped, Jingles babbled without cease. By late afternoon, I was fully informed on subjects as diverse and dubious as the native savages being the Lost Tribe of Israel; the care and feeding of pachyderms, canaries, and camels; the proper weaving of Navajo blankets and the nurture of Apache boys; the Mexican War, in which I gathered he had played some role; and the life and times of a lawman named Wyatt Earp, including those of his many brothers and associates.

This last part I had some interest in, because one of Earp's closest companions was Doc Holiday. The stories Jingles told were quite different from the one in my book, however, and I didn't know which to believe.

There may have been other topics, but frankly, I can't remember them. Jingles was inexhaustible. Cole didn't even attempt to get a word in edgewise, and I was limited to an occasional "Really?" or "My goodness." Lop Ear's comments filled in the lulls, although they were far too few.

It was nearly nightfall when we traversed the last brushy valley and came upon the Aztec Princess. Jingles, without being warned, halted his jangling wagon and team a good distance away.

"I'm not goin' to take a chance on winding up in one of those sinkholes, no, sir," he said as he climbed down from his wagon. "We have had them in Tombstone, too, right smack in town. Miracle they got the horses out. Roan and a nice buckskin, as I remember. You sure you got no bats?"

"No bats." I had already reassured him countless

times there was not one single bat in the Aztec Princess to the best of my knowledge.

"Can't be too careful about bats," he said.

My head was still ringing, and I rubbed at my ear as he began to unharness the team. The others had ridden ahead, but I lingered.

"I've been meaning to ask you, Jingles," I said, probably a bit louder than necessary. "Why on earth do you want such a noisy wagon?"

"Apache," he replied, and slid me a conspiratorial glance, as if this should say it all.

But it didn't, and I asked, "What about Apache?"

He had just pulled the cotton from Gracie's ears. As she made an abortive attempt to take a bite out of his leg, he said, "Why, they're afraid of the noise! They think it's ghosts coming. I am not bothered by Apache anymore, I can tell you that much. Keep your choppers to yourself, pusscat."

Grace groaned and sat down, and I leaned on my saddle horn. "But Cole told me the Apache have all been rounded up. I don't see why—"

"You never can tell when one of those devils is goin' to jump the reservation, young Tate Horace Smith Donovan, or whatever your name is," he said, leading Comanche from the traces. That poor sorrel looked more swaybacked every time I looked at him. If you had balanced a straight board from his withers to his croup, I honestly believe the drop from the plank to his sagging topline would have been a good two feet.

"I figure to be prepared, that's all," he continued. "I have had my run-ins with Apache—yessirree, Bob—and I do not care to repeat the experience. Now, when I know you better, I will tell you the story about how I came to get my gold bar."

And then, although the swayback gave no visible sign whatsoever of a change in attitude—his eyes were, in fact, half lidded—Jingles suddenly took a firm hold on his bridle.

"Easy, boy! Down, I say!" He turned to me and hissed, "You'd best ride on down after the others. My Comanche is getting worked up, and you do not want to be around when a foul mood strikes him."

Although I was mildly intrigued by that gold bar, I had already learned not to press Jingles. Any questions were liable to lead into a dislocated tangle of how to trim a burro's hooves or mule skinning on the Santa Fe trail or somesuch, and never get back to the point. So I touched the brim of my hat and clucked to Tell.

Later that evening, Jingles and Lop Ear and Cole lit candles and went down the shaft to have a look. I stayed up top with the horses and Loretta. I'd had enough of mine shafts already, and didn't see any point on trudging down into that claustrophobic—and snake-infested—darkness when I didn't absolutely have to.

They were down there quite some time, during which I called Loretta to me and started making her over to pass the time. She really was quite a nice dog, once you got past her looks, and she seemed more than appreciative of the attention. I even went to my packs, dug out the body brush I used on Tell, and gave her a good going-over.

Oh, she loved that! The hair and burrs and nettles fairly flew, and with them a good bit of dirt that had me sneezing. She closed her eyes and stretched out her neck, and made all sorts of contented moans and whines and what I can only describe as gurgles, and leaned into the brush so hard that had I not physically held her up, she would have toppled over.

I was just looking her over, amazed at the transformation a little elbow grease had achieved, when she suddenly ceased licking me and stared off into the distance. A low growl, which I felt through her body more than heard, rose up in her, and she stiffened. I threw my arm over her shoulders and across her chest to hold her back—from what, I didn't know— and looked in the direction that seemed to disturb her.

The moon was fairly bright that night, but all I could see, other than the night-silvered shapes of the fallen building, the old pump, and the surrounding vegetation were the shadows of two of those gaping holes, where the mine had caved in on itself.

Loretta's growl rose audibly. She lunged forward, but I caught her before she had gone an inch and hugged her tighter. Whatever was out there, I didn't wish Loretta, brave thing, to fall victim to it.

And just then, I saw it. A shadow at the edge of one of the holes in the ground, the one farthest from me. Well, it wasn't a separate shadow at first. It was more like the hole was suddenly growing, had come alive, like something out of an Edgar Allan Poe tale. All the hairs on the back of my neck stood up, and I swallowed hard. But then the swell of black suddenly separated from the main of the hole, and moonlight eerily struck a bobcat's silhouette.

Abruptly, Loretta burst into a frenzy of furious barks that nearly deafened me. I must have loosened my grip on her, because she gave a tremendous push and vaulted through the ring made by my neck and my restraining arm and shoulder. The bobcat sprinted away with Loretta hard on its heels.

They were out of site in a nonce, and I didn't realize until they disappeared that Loretta had very nearly broken my jaw.

We rose with the sun the next morning and bid a hasty goodbye to Jingles and Lop Ear, who were happily unloading explosives from the wagon when I lost sight of them. Loretta, back from her late-night cat chase and, full of new burrs and grit, stood atop the wagon seat, overseeing.

"Are you certain they're entirely trustworthy?" I asked Cole. The question had plagued me for days, but it was the first chance I'd had to be alone with Cole. Frankly, I was certain that Jingles, although well intentioned, was half mad. I wasn't too sure about Lop Ear's sanity, either.

But Cole only scowled at me. I was becoming adept at reading those scowls and grimaces, though. This one said, "Don't be an idiot." Well, it was probably phrased a bit rougher than that, but I got the gist of it, and didn't ask him again. If he trusted those two old coots, I supposed I had no other choice but to go along with him.

We rode on in blessed silence, free from ringing and jangling and wagon thuds, punctuated only by the gentle scrapes of horse legs against brush, the soft creaking of saddle leather, and the occasional clatter of a bit against teeth. In fact, neither of us spoke another word until Cole called a halt at noon.

We watered the horses, and around a mouthful of jerky, Cole, completely out of the blue, asked, "You wantin' to learn to use that pistol?"

The question startled me, but not enough to keep me from nodding eagerly. "Yes! Certainly!"

He motioned me to follow, and walked about twenty feet away from the horses. We were well out of those hills now and on the flat, where the growth was all thigh-high scrub and tall cactus with wide, twisty, gravelly bare spaces in between. He pointed to a large prickly pear about fifty feet away.

Still chewing his jerky, he pushed back his hat. "See if you can manage to hit that, Donovan."

I tucked my jerky into my pocket, drew my revolver, and rotated the chambers so that the hammer rested on a full one. Then I raised my gun with both hands, closed one eye, and sighted down on the cactus.

"Hold it," he snapped before I had a chance to pull the trigger.

The gun sagged in my hands.

"One hand," he said.

"It's heavy!"

"You'll get used to it. Jesus."

One-handed, I raised the pistol once more. Again, I closed one eye and sighted on the cactus.

But just as I was about to pull the trigger, he said, "Wait!"

Exasperated, I said, "*Now* what!"

"Keep both your eyes open, boy."

"Why?"

He growled, "Because I said so."

I arched my brows, hoping he would notice what pains he was putting me to. But he didn't, so I sighed and raised the gun again.

This time, I pulled the trigger.

The gun jumped in my hand with such explosive force that I nearly dropped it. And worse, the cactus seemed to have suffered no damage whatsoever.

I was fully prepared to endure Cole's laughter, but all he said was, "Squeeze that trigger real easy, kid. Don't yank it."

I sighted and tried again.

This time I did better. I was prepared for the kick

of the gun, and this time I gently squeezed the trigger. A pad on the left-hand side flew into the air! Of course, I had been aiming for the center, and this particular clump of prickly pear was perhaps eight feet wide, but I felt a thrill of accomplishment in having hit it at all.

Grinning, I turned to Cole. His face was void of expression, which took some of the wind out of my sails. He said, "Again."

He never asked me what part I was aiming at, which was just as well because I never hit my selected target dead on. But by the time I'd fired the fifth bullet from my trusty Colt, I was within a foot of my mark.

"Fair," he said, turning back toward the horses. "We'll try again tonight."

We did. In fact, from then on, he let me practice every chance we got. I got better, if I do say so myself, and by the last time we practiced, just before we rode back into Tonto's Wickiup, I was drawing from the holster and firing in a reasonably smooth manner, and managed to puncture a hole less than a half foot from where I was aiming. Give or take an inch or two.

I was proud of myself. I was also aware that Cole wasn't doing this just to be nice, although he didn't offer his reasons. Oh, I knew that he felt bad about what had happened in Poco Bueno with John Henry Strider. I thought that Cole, in some sort of lopsided fashion, was trying to make it up to me.

But it dawned on me, when I was dozing off that first night, that Cole was readying me to face that which he was certain was coming—every quick-draw Johnny, as he had put it, in the territory.

I didn't really believe this would happen, if truth be told. After all, once I was back in Tonto's Wickiup, I would wrench my own name back into place and take care of this Donovan business. No one, I was certain, would think to look for me at Hanratty's.

We had Tonto's Wickiup in sight, on the distant, flat horizon, when I finally asked Cole the question. I had thought how to work up to it over the last day, but it still took a great deal of throat clearing to muster the courage to start.

"Somethin' wrong with your lungs, kid?" Cole asked me.

"N-nothing," I said as I got hold of myself. "I was just wondering . . . that is . . ."

"Spit it out," he grumbled.

"Why did someone shoot your horse out from under you?" There. It was finally out, at least the first part of it. "When you were up north, seeing about Uncle Hector, I mean."

"I know what you mean," he snapped. "It ain't like somebody drops my pony every other Tuesday." He took a moment to pat Ranger's neck, and then he looked over at me again for a long time before he said, "I don't know. But I'm thinkin' it was on account of the mine. Your mine."

"My copper mine?" Frankly, I was puzzled. Why

on earth would anybody shoot Cole's horse over a copper mine that was barely breaking even?

"No, the Aztec Princess. Now Heck didn't say a word to nobody. He could keep a secret, all right, so I can't figure how anybody would have known about it." He reined in Ranger and sat there, his palms pressed into the saddle's horn. "But somehow somebody found out. And they killed him for it. Tried to kill me, too. Missed and hit Brownie instead."

"But why on earth would someone . . . ?"

"Kid, I don't know." He shook his head. "It's just . . . well, I can't figure any other reason anybody'd have to give old Heck a shove down that shaft, that's all. Everybody liked Heck."

I didn't argue with him, but it seemed to me that he was just guessing, both about Uncle Hector's "murder" and the reasoning for it. There was no need for me to embarrass myself any further. I simply nodded, said, "Thank you, Cole," and rode on.

Riding in silence once again, we came into town and were most of the way to the livery stable when my life changed. That was when I first saw her, you see, there on the walk in front of the milliner's shop, and instantly knew she would be the one. She was small and blond, with the face of an angel: bee-stung lips, a pert little nose, and big blue eyes, bright with intelligence and twinkling with humor.

I nearly fell from the saddle, and in fact, Cole reached out and grasped my arm. "You all right, boy?" he asked. "Your color's off."

I shook off his hand and pointed to the sidewalk, asking, "Who is that girl? The one with the older woman." I had guessed the latter to be her mother and had already wondered whether she would approve of her daughter marrying the local whoremaster.

"Those gals in front of the hat shop?" Cole said. "That's Mrs. O'Brien and one of her daughters. They've got about ten of 'em, I reckon. I think that one's Annie. Third from the oldest. Their oldest girl, Jane, she's teachin' in the school now. Why?"

By this time, we had ridden past the milliner's shop, and I was turned halfway round in my saddle, staring. Annie glanced up, and without knowing it, I raised a hand in greeting. She smiled and daintily waved a delicate hand to me before her mother spoke to her, distracting her attention.

I righted myself in the saddle. Cole was staring at me, expecting an answer to his inquiry.

"Because I'm going to marry her," I said. And that was that. Some things, you just know.

14

After settling the horses at the livery, we started up the street toward Hanratty's, carrying our saddlebags and pack rolls. Cole finally spoke. "Marry her?" he said, with a twinkle in his eye.

I felt heat creeping up my neck, and snapped, "I don't appreciate being the brunt of your private jest, sir." I already regretted blurting out my intentions, but it was too late to take the words back. The intentions, however, I wished to stand by. Just not to Cole.

Cole laughed softly, but didn't press the point.

We were about a foot from Hanratty's swinging doors when I heard a shot, and at the same time felt my ear sting. I must say that I didn't put the two together. I simply slapped a hand to my bloody ear, insulted that in addition to venomous snakes and spiders, Arizona had boy-biting bees!

Cole put a hand to my shoulder and shoved me through the batwing doors before I had a chance to remark on it, though. I landed on the floor in a heap, and watched as, beneath the doors, Cole's belongings dropped to the sidewalk and his booted feet took off, toward the sound of the shot.

And then Belle was at my side, wailing, "What happened? You're hurt! Where's Cole!"

I do not remember if I answered, for I had just then realized that someone had shot at me—at me!—and scrambled backward, across the floor, until the stairway's first step pressed into the small of my back.

Belle pressed a damp bar towel to the side of my head, and repeated, "Where's Cole?"

Just then, two more shots split the air, fired in rapid succession. Then a third!

Belle rose to her feet, crying, "My God, Cole! What is it?"

It was then I knew that Belle would not keep me from my Anne. It was Cole and Cole alone she loved. There was a tinge of sadness upon my heart, but also joy. Now nothing stood between me and Anne— other than the fact that she had never met me, of course.

And I must admit, with a great deal of shame, that it was only then that I came to my senses and realized that Cole had more than likely gone to apprehend whoever it was who had fired at me. He was out there, protecting me with his own life! I tried to spring to my feet without much success, but on the third try, I made it. With Belle screaming for me to come back, I rushed to the doors and pushed through, to the sidewalk.

Cole was nowhere in sight. I started up the street in the direction he'd taken—trembling hand on the butt of my gun, fear so thick in my veins that it was a wonder I could walk at all, and clinging close to the storefronts. There was no one else around, but a hint of movement behind the window of a store across the way told me that everyone had gone inside.

To hide, no doubt. It seemed as if the entire town had suddenly been lifted into Glory.

Which was exactly what was going to happen to me, if I wasn't careful. But by the time I managed to drag my trembling form one block, I saw a man's shadow, up ahead, emerging from the mouth of an alley.

Cole had trained me well. I "skinned leather" and smoothly drew—and just stopped myself from firing in time. The man was Cole, and he was holstering his gun.

I stood there, frozen into place, while he walked the two blocks between us. Up and down the street, doors slowly creaked open. Shouts of "Everything all right, Jeffries?" and "What the hell's goin' on out there?" rang through the streets.

Cole, still walking, called to one man, "Get the sheriff, Red. Undertaker, too, I reckon." His face was deadly serious.

Red, whoever he was, ran up the street and out of

sight at about the time Cole reached me. He gave me a long stare and said, "Thought I shoved you outta harm's way, kid."

I squared my shoulders. "Only for so long. And I'm not a kid."

"Remains to be seen," he muttered, and pushed past me.

I followed him into Hanratty's, and slouched beside him when he pulled out a chair at Uncle Hector's special table. "Beer," he shouted to Willie, just as Belle joined us.

"I was so worried!" she murmured, and started to fawn over him. "Who was it this time, Cole? The Blakely brothers? Seth Thompson? I heard he was headed down this way."

"Wasn't me they were shootin' at." He pulled his watch from its pocket. "Walt Eli must be out to lunch." He glanced at me, and added, "Eli's the law around Tonto's Wickiup, such as it is," before he turned to Belle again and shook his head. "Ol' Walt probably dived under the table the second he heard them shots."

At that moment, the sheriff—dark, shortish, and husky—pushed his way through the doors and approached us. "Miss Belle," he said, touching the brim of his hat, then immediately focused his attention on Cole. "What did you ever to do Big Johnny Hill to make him mad enough to take a shot at you? More to the point, what'd you do to whoever hired him?"

Cole's beer appeared at about that time, and he

took a long drink before he said, "Damned if I know, Walt. I 'specially don't know what this boy, here, did to get him riled."

The sheriff suddenly took a good look at me and said, "You're bleedin', boy!"

"Willie, I forgot," the negligent Belle piped up. "Go get Doc Hastings."

Cole briefly capsulized what had happened—while I marveled that Belle could have forgotten I was injured—and then he came to the part I didn't know. It seemed that this Big John Hill character was a wanted gunman, one who hired himself out, usually to someone who wished somebody else dead. Cole remarked that Hill had thirty-three notches on his gun. Sheriff Eli remarked that it was a "pure-D miracle" that it wasn't thirty-four, to which Cole replied that he knew what he was doing, thank you very much.

I had no reason to doubt him, although the sheriff just shrugged. My anger with Cole over the mines and Lop Ear and Jingles had transformed back into the admiration I had once held for him. He had saved my life, and I was grateful.

The doctor came and patched my ear, remarking that it was "goddamn miraculous" I hadn't been killed. As it was, a small piece had been nicked from the upper cartilage, so my ear, if you looked at it closely, would forever have a notched appearance. All in all, however, it was a very small thing.

After the wound was cauterized—a much more painful procedure than the original injury, I assure you—I went back downstairs. Hanratty's had opened for the day during my absence, and the customers were already two and three deep at the bar. Cole was still slouched at Uncle Hector's private table—sans the sheriff—and the lovely Belle was nowhere in sight.

I strolled over to Cole, dodging two miners and a cowhand along the way, and sat down.

Cole looked up from his beer. "Why ain't you in bed?" he asked.

"I wasn't hurt that badly. Cole, I want to go up to the Lucky Seven."

"What the hell for? You aimin' to get yourself killed for real this time?"

I sighed. "Cole, two men have come after me in the past four days. I don't know why, because you keep killing them before they can be questioned. I want to find out why."

He glowered at me, but said nothing, for just then, Belle joined us.

She flounced down onto his lap, said, "Hiya, Horace!" to me, and planted a kiss on Cole's lips. It lasted a considerable time.

Again, I felt a pull toward Belle, but this time, it was with nostalgia, of all things. The beautiful Anne awaited me, after all. I filed Belle in the past with the other silly, overreaching, and ludicrous dreams of my childhood, and decided to concentrate on my future. I would be serious. I would be steadfast. And I wanted to get this thing cleared up before I brought my sweet Annie O'Brien into it.

Already, she was "my sweet Annie."

"You're liable to get yourself dead, kid," Cole said.

I thought quickly. "Not if you come along!"

"Whoa!" said Belle. "Just what are you boys up to now?"

Before Cole had a chance to answer, I said, "I'm attempting to learn who is trying to kill me, Belle, and why."

Her brow furrowed. "Kill you? I thought it was Cole that Big John Hill was after!"

Grudgingly, Cole said, "No, Belle. I'm afraid he was after Donovan, here. And we ran into John Henry Strider a coupla days ago. He was ready to gun down the kid, too."

I said, "Then you're just as puzzled as I, Cole?"

He stared at his half-empty beer mug for a second, then said, "All right, yeah, I am."

"John Henry Strider?" Belle cried, loud enough that a few men turned their heads our way. "John Henry Strider's out after Horace, too?"

"Was," I said. "Cole killed him, although I got the blame."

"Cole . . ." she began, but he hushed her.

"Let's talk about this upstairs, honey," he urged as he stood up.

She stood up, too, saying, "Horace, don't you set one blasted foot outside! You hear me?"

"Yes, Belle," I said. I had no intention of going through Hanratty's doors again. At least, not until we set out for the Lucky Seven.

Once Belle and Cole had gone upstairs and closed the door behind them, it occurred to me that it might be a smart, although not honorable, idea to go upstairs, too, and listen to their conversation.

I had a brief tussle with myself over this, but in the end, intelligence won out over ideals, and I climbed the stairs. I quickly made my way to the bedroom, wrestled off my boots, and lay on the bed, my good ear to the wall.

"Well, how did Strider know who he was?" Belle was demanding.

"Because the little idiot told him," Cole replied curtly, and I flushed with shame. It is one thing to hear someone call you an idiot to your face, but another entirely to overhear it said to another person. Especially to one you like.

Belle muttered something I couldn't make out, and then Cole answered, "I don't know, honey. I don't know why the hell Strider was lookin' for him, and I can't figure Hill, either. Unless it has somethin' to do with the mine."

"What mine?"

"Never mind. C'mere."

"Don't try to pretty talk me, Cole Jeffries! What's going on?"

"Belle." He sighed. "I can't tell you. I promised the kid, okay?"

Of all the times to keep his word, after he'd told nearly everyone else in the territory!

And Belle didn't press him, drat her! She said, "All right, Cole Jeffries. I'm letting you off the hook, just this once."

Afterward, there was no more conversation, just the sounds of grown-up things taking place, so I went back out to my parlor, sank down in the leather chair, and slept.

I awakened to the thuds of a fist pounding on my door, and realized that I had slept through the afternoon and the night in Uncle Hector's chair. Morning was just breaking outside my windows when I groggily called, "Just a minute!"

Cole, fully dressed, was at my door. "Well?" he demanded.

I ground fists into my eyes. "Well, what?"

"Thought you wanted to take a ride up to the Lucky Seven."

"Now?"

"Good a time as any," he said as he turned toward the landing. "C'mon, kid. Get a move on."

We traveled to the northwest, and by dusk, we found ourselves just outside the beehive of activity that was the Lucky Seven mine. It was, as Cole said, a full-tilt operation, with a smelter, barracks for the miners, a cookhouse, and other assorted buildings, even a small church. Men were everywhere, whistles blew, dogs and burros and goats meandered through the crowd of grubby miners coming off shift and the slightly cleaner ones starting to work.

The landscape had grown quite hilly for the last few miles, and the main shaft of the Lucky Seven started in the top of the highest hill I'd seen thus far, and went straight down. I say this, because there was a cage of sorts, rigged to go up and down in the mine on a series of chains. It was powered by a trio of mules who walked round and round, turning a giant spindle, which lowered the cage. When they wanted to bring someone up, an employee would go fuss with the rigging, and the mules would start walking again. I was fascinated to see how it worked!

Cole and I rode directly up to a door at the end of a long building, and dismounted. There was a small sign that said, LUCKY SEVEN ENTERPRISES, HECTOR PEMBERTON, PROPRIETOR.

Cole tossed his reins over the rail. I did, too, and followed him through the door and into what proved to be the office.

A harried-looking man sat at the desk, hunched over a ledger. He looked up quickly, frowned, and thumbed his visor back a hair. "You again?" he growled at Cole. "What now?"

"Brought the new owner up to inspect the place, Trimble, and nice to see you, too. You find Heck's body, yet?"

The clerk's frown deepened, but he stood up and reached a limp hand over the desk. I took it, saying,

"Horace Tate Pemberton Smith, at your service, sir," and gave it a firm shake.

"You think you got enough names, kid?" he said, pulling away. He stuck his hand under his armpit and added, "That's quite the handshake you got there."

"Just call him Donovan," Cole said. His eyes narrowed, and he looked straight at Mr. Trimble. "Now about Heck . . ."

Cole had a way with people. Pretty soon, Mr. Trimble was disgorging more information than anyone needed to know. They had found Uncle Hector's body—much the worse for wear, I imagined—and they had also come across a fresh vein of copper ore. The crew was mining this now. Trimble had, indeed, also seen a man of Big John Hill's description around the site at the time of Uncle Hector's death, and after, when Cole had come up to see about him. And had his poor horse shot from beneath him.

"It's a puzzlement, kid," Cole said to me, once we'd walked a distance from the camp and the sun was going down. "I'll be hanged for a chicken thief if Hill wasn't the rat bastard what gave ol' Heck a shove down the shaft, and killed my Brownie horse, too. But . . ." He threw up his hands, then pulled out his tobacco pouch and proceeded to roll himself a cigarette.

He pulled a match from his tin and flicked it to life. "This whole thing is way beyond me," he said around the smoke he was lighting. "C'mon, kid. You're the one with all that fancy education. You got any ideas?"

I shrugged. I honestly didn't have a clue.

That night, Cole and I slept apart from the others—which meant on the ground, ringed by our ropes. I had barely nodded off when I thought I heard a familiar voice.

Willie? Willie from Hanratty's?

I opened my eyes and sat up.

"Cole?" the voice came again, in an exaggerated stage whisper. "Cole! Horace! Shit, I mean, Tate! You out here?"

I stood up and whispered, "Willie?" into the darkness.

I heard stumbling feet approaching, then made out Willie's bulky form emerging from the darkness. I waved a hand, and whispered, "Willie, over here!"

"Thank God," he muttered. "Bad enough I gotta ride up here, half in the dark." He neared and stopped, facing me. "Worse still that you two lunatics had to sleep on the ground instead of in a nice building. With lamps 'n' candles." He paused to dig through his pockets, during which time, Cole came awake.

"What!" he said, jumping to his feet and drawing his gun all at the same time.

"No need for theatrics," I said, with a touch of superiority. "It's Willie. From Hanratty's."

"I know where he's from," Cole snarled before he turned to our visitor. "What is it, Willie? Somethin' wrong with Belle?"

"Naw," Willie grumbled. "Got a wire for the . . . Got a wire for Horace—I mean Tate." He produced a crumpled wad of paper and held it out. "Belle thought it might be important."

I took it and smoothed it, a feat that took no small amount of time.

"You rode up here in the middle of the night?" Cole was asking.

"It was light when I started out," Willie said defensively. "Ain't my fault. You know how Belle is, Cole, when she gets an idea in her head 'bout something."

I looked up from the telegram, which I was squinting at in the moonlight. It was nothing, after all. "It's all right," I said, folded the mangled paper, and tucked it in my pocket. "Just a wire from Mr. Aloysius Dean, Father's attorney." I believe I said it a bit grandly, as if Mr. Dean were my attorney, as well. Which I suppose he was.

As one, Willie and Cole said, "Well?"

I blinked. "What?"

They looked at each other, and then Cole said, "A man rode near thirty miles, some of it in the dark, to bring you that paper. Least you can do is to read it to him! Ain't you got no manners?"

I snapped, "Of course I do!" although I didn't add that I failed to see the sharing of private information as socially relevant. Additionally, I had no wish to share it, for Mr. Dean had wired to ask me how much money I needed.

I continued. "Mr. Dean asks after my health and wonders if Uncle Hector is doing right by me, that's all."

Willie scowled. "Well, why the hell couldn't he put that in a regular letter, 'stead of gettin' everybody all riled up?"

Cole put his hand on Willie's shoulder. "I reckon everything's a big emergency to New York City folks, Willie. You want to bed down with us? You had any chuck yet?"

While they talked, I wandered across the camp to a torch left blazing before one of the buildings. In its unsteady light, I once again read the wire, then again. I supposed I would have to share it with Cole, after all. Not that I really had a reason to keep it to myself, but one likes to think one has some bits of discretion left, even if they're nonsensical.

And besides, perhaps Cole would know how much cash would be required. Or at least, he would be able to communicate with Lop Ear and Jingles, something I feared myself inadequate to do.

Understand anything that came out of their mouths, I mean.

I tucked the telegram away and picked my way back to my bedroll. Apparently Cole had rustled up something from the cookhouse, because Willie was fully occupied with a plate heaped with something roughly resembling food. I sat down on my blankets, after giving them a quick kick in case of snakes.

"You're learnin', kid," Cole muttered.

I made no response, either to the "you're learning" or the "kid." I simply eased my head down upon my saddle and closed my eyes, and let my thoughts ramble pleasantly from Annie to my impending riches and back to Annie, until I nodded off.

I learned very little at the Lucky Seven, aside from the fact that Uncle Hector's body had been swiftly buried again once it was rescued, and that I could count on a small income from the mine itself. For an undisclosed period, at any rate.

However, I did not think the copper income would be nearly sufficient to cover the costs of reopening the Aztec Princess. That was the preeminent matter weighing upon my mind. After we paid our respects at Uncle Hector's grave, we bade Mr. Trimble goodbye and rode out of the camp, and Cole said, "How's it feel?"

"How's what feel? Uncle Hector, you mean?"

"Realizin' all those boys back there depend on you for a paycheck," he said.

I hadn't honestly thought about it, not like that. To tell the truth, I hadn't really given much thought to all those buildings, all that livestock, and all those men, well, being my responsibility. After a pause, I said, "It is quite a commitment."

I glanced back, to where Willie was riding, and deemed him far enough away to be out of hearing range. "Cole, Mr. Dean wishes to know how much money will be needed to put the Aztec Princess in operation once more."

"Dean? The telegram Dean?"

I nodded and he snapped, "How the hell does he know anything about it?"

I was taken a bit aback, but replied, "Well, *you* told everyone that would hold still! I sent one wire— that was all."

"From where?" he demanded. "Where were we that had a telegraph office, Horace?"

His use of my correct name sent chills through my limbs, and I meekly replied, "Tombstone?"

He made a sound I cannot describe, but one I took to be intended to denote his total disgust, and he lashed Ranger with his reins. They sprinted out ahead a good fifty yards before Cole reined the horse back down to a walk.

I held Tell back, although he was game. If a little thing like this could put Cole into such a foul mood, I had no intentions of keeping pace with him. Let him sulk on his own, I thought. Let me play the part of adult.

I could almost hear Cole's voice adding, in my head, *For a change.*

15

We were roughly ten miles from Phoenix when Willie, who at that time was riding off my left, exclaimed, "Where the hell's he goin'?"

"Why?" I asked. I had noticed that Cole, far up ahead, had veered off to the right, but I imagined that he knew where he was headed. This land all looked the same to me.

"Because he ain't goin' back to Tonto's Wickiup, that's why," Willie said and kicked his horse ahead, apparently intending to catch up with Cole, which he did in a moment.

Once again, I held my Tell back. I wasn't sure that I wanted to talk to Cole yet. I had been rolling his actions around in my mind, and frankly, I was irritated with his attitude! It was my mine, wasn't it? I surely had more business telling Mr. Dean—who might be of some financial use—about the strike than

Cole had telling Jingles Beldon, the dynamiting, bell-ringing, camel-grooming king of the territory!

I watched while Cole and Willie appeared to hold a discussion. Then Willie came back onto the trail that we had been following—which would take us back to Tonto's Wickiup—and pushed his horse into a soft lope. I decided I had best find out what was going on, and despite my misgivings, I determined to check with Cole first.

After all, I reasoned, he had brought me.

So I urged Tell forward, and caught Cole in an instant. When I reached him and slowed down to ride alongside, though, he didn't acknowledge my presence.

"Cole?"

He still stared straight ahead, through his horse's ears.

I reached over and grabbed his shoulder. *"Cole!"* I repeated, half shouting.

At last, he acknowledged that I was breathing, if only with a curt nod. Still, it was something.

"Where are you going? Why is Willie going back to town alone?"

His jaw muscles worked for a long moment before he said, "Gotta talk to you, Donovan." He suddenly twisted toward me and snapped, "And don't tell me not to call you Donovan!"

After that outburst, I was almost afraid to prod him for more information—let alone correct him—and waited a good minute before I spoke again. "Well, I'm here, Cole. Go ahead and talk."

"Not now, kid. Not until I get a couple drinks in me, anyhow."

"What?"

He pointed up ahead. I saw a small cluster of shacks huddled on the horizon. "What is it?"

He said, "Whiskey," and pushed Ranger into a gallop.

Leave it to Cole to find a saloon in the middle of nowhere, I thought.

I had no choice but to follow.

Fifteen minutes later, we were seated in the shade of a rough saguaro-rib ramada, and Cole was tossing back his third shot of red-eye whiskey. The man in charge, one Lucius J. Crooke, seemed impressed with my being the owner of Hanratty's, and kept prodding me with nonsensical or plainly stupid questions, always followed by "You know, businessman to businessman?"

While I tried to keep Mr. Crooke entertained until Cole was well oiled enough to speak his mind to me, I noted the other patrons. Both were seated deeper inside the ramada, in purple shade, but I made out two men, I thought, in opposite corners. One seemed a rough sort, the other a bit more cultured. I discerned this by looking at their boots, mind you. The toes of them were the only parts I could truly make out with any clarity.

Cole ordered himself a beer, this time, and added, "Give him one, too, Lucius."

When I declined it, he pressed the point, and I actually had to drink half of the warm brew before he was satisfied. I was not, however. There was a dead fly floating in it.

Cole waved Mr. Crooke off and leaned across the three-legged table, toward me. "All right, kid. I hope I got enough whiskey in me to hold me from swattin' you clean to Mexico." He stopped a moment to clear his throat. "You sent a telegram back east, the day we left Tombstone, right?"

I was still back on the part where I went to Mexico, powered by the force of one of his fists, and it took me a second to say, "Y-yes. Yes, I did."

"And you been tellin' everybody your real name's Horace Tate Whatever, even though I told you a dozen times to stick with Tate Donovan?"

"But I don't see what that has to do with—"

Something bumped my chair, and I looked up to see a rather large man standing at my shoulder. A quick glance down at his boots told me he was one of the fellows who had been seated in the shadows. The rough one. "You Horace Smith?" he asked, although it emerged as more of a growl.

I nodded, unsure of what to make of him.

He turned his attention to Cole, who was sliding out of his chair to stand. "You Cole Jeffries?" he grumbled again.

"What about it?" Cole replied, and I heard a dare in his voice. Frankly, at that moment, I was terrified of both of them.

"I'm Duffer Atbrun," the man said with a scowl as he stared at Cole. "Old John Hill was a friend o' mine, and you're the one what dropped him."

"Only after he nearly dropped me!" I heard myself saying, and slapped a hand over my own mouth, too late.

For at that second, one of Duff Atbrun's hamlike hands shoved me out of my chair, to the ground, and with his other, he drew his gun.

Thank God that Cole was faster! I heard two shots, so close in succession that one might have been the echo of the other, and Duff Atbrun fell to his knees.

He wasn't dead quite yet, though, and he twisted to point his gun at me. More from training and instinct than any sense of bravery, I drew and fired, only realizing afterward that it was a living man I was shooting at, not a cactus.

But Atbrun tumbled, nonetheless. He went over backward and lay still.

I was still, too—frozen into place by the fact of what I had just done. *Oh, dear Mother and Father*, I remember thinking, *thank the Lord you're dead so I won't have to tell you about this!*

"Couldn'ta done that if he hadn't been drinkin' all afternoon," said Lucius Crooke, breaking the silence. "Hell, I didn't even know he could wobble up!"

Cole holstered his gun and came round the table. He kicked Atbrun's gun clear of his hand before he said, "Lucius, did you know he was gunnin' for me?"

Mr. Crooke shrank back somewhat under the blistering heat of Cole's accusatory tone, but he said, "Can't say as I did, Cole. He were madder than a bagful o' badgers when he rode in, but he didn't share no names with me."

Cole snorted. "Christ, Lucius, you coulda warned me. When's his lordship get back, anyway?"

Lucius shrugged. "Don't know. He's passed out." He indicated the second man in the shadows, the one with nicer boots.

I shook off the last of my paralysis, holstered my weapon, and said, "His lordship?"

"Forgot you were down there, kid," Cole said, and gave me a hand up. "His lordship's the proprietor of this ramshackle excuse for a saloon. Lord Daryl Duppa, that is."

"A real lord?" I had never heard anything so fantastic in my life as a real lord living practically on the open prairie!

"That's up for discussion," Cole said, and righted his chair. Atbrun's right leg had knocked it over when he toppled.

"No, son, he's a real one," Lucius said quickly. "English. His family, they pays him to stay over here, 'cross the pond."

"Oh," I said, staring at the corpse. I vaguely recalled hearing of such bounders as Duppa, ne'er-do-well shirttail royals whose families doled them out an allowance, so long as they didn't go back to England and embarrass the old coat of arms. But right at the moment, I was more concerned with the body, and the fact that I'd changed it from a living man into a deceased one.

Lucius was pouring Cole another beer. I said, "Shouldn't someone . . . do something about him?" Neither Cole nor Lucius nor the man passed out in the shadows seemed the least bit concerned about him. In fact, Lucius stepped casually over the body to bring Cole his beer.

"Oh, too hot to do any diggin' now," Lucius said. "He'll keep till the sun goes down."

Cole said nothing, just tipped back his beer and took a long drink.

"You'll read the Bible over him?" I asked.

"Why?" Cole interjected before Lucius had a chance to answer. "You think that'll iron the wrinkles out of you killin' him? Or get him in good with God?"

Actually, I think I did. I shrank down in my seat and stared at my hands.

"From now on, kid, you listen to me, and you pay attention," he continued. His tone indicated that if I had ever listened to anyone, I should now be doubly heedful. And I was. "You will not tell anybody else about this Horace shit. That's ended right this minute. Got that?"

I nodded, vaguely offended. "Yessir."

"You won't send anymore goddamn telegrams or letters, not even to the Queen of England!"

"I don't see why I'd have any call to—"

"Shut up! Dad blast you, Donovan! You have a real goddamn knack for stirrin' up trouble," he shouted, "and by trouble, I mean gettin' people killed!" He kicked the late Mr. Atbrun's rib cage for emphasis, and a small cloud of dust rose from the corpse's vest.

"Yessir," I said, cowed. He'd made his point.

"I don't know how much trouble you dragged up, but I got a feelin' this is only the start of it, kid. From now on, you do what I say and *only* what I say— you got that?"

I nodded.

Cole seemed reasonably satisfied, and turned his attention to his beer and away from me.

I was glad.

We left the cluster of ramadas and lean-tos behind before dark—and therefore before anyone started digging a last resting place for the late Mr. Atbrun— and headed back toward Tonto's Wickiup. I cannot say that Cole was in an improved temper, but at least he had enough liquor in him that he didn't hit me. Nor did he preach at me anymore. He just rode on in silence, and I followed suit.

We came into Tonto's Wickiup just past sunset, and we were back at Hanratty's, which, at only seven thirty, was filled almost to the rafters. After I placed a dinner order with the mysterious Ma—I had yet to discern whose mother she really was—and tipped my hat to Belle, I went on up to my rooms.

I was exhausted. In the space of less than forty-eight hours, I had been shot in the ear, killed a man who pointed a gun at me, been offered a great deal of cash by Mr. Dean, discovered what had become of Uncle Hector, and learned that my copper mine would support me for a little while longer. And my ear still hurt.

Well, Mr. Dean hadn't exactly offered me cash. At least, it was not a firm deal as yet. And I hadn't had a chance to ask Cole about it. Not that I would have asked, even if I'd had a chance. I didn't dare make him angry again.

As I sat in Uncle Hector's leather chair, waiting for my dinner, I couldn't cleanse my mind of one image: the face of Mr. Atbrun, as he fell that last time. He had looked surprised, I recalled. He had looked as if he couldn't believe he had been killed by a child, and as if he was offended by the fact!

As awful as I felt about having pulled the trigger, and as appalled as I was about what I perceived to be his reaction to my doing so, I found his attitude somewhat . . . off-putting. I cannot explain it better than that, other than to say it made my stomach queasy and my sense of right and wrong seem somehow tilted. It just didn't fit together—at least, not in any sense to which I was accustomed.

Willie was the one who delivered my supper, and I ate it alone, and deep in thought. I managed, somewhere during the entrée, to turn my thoughts to the charming and beautiful Annie O'Brien. I imagined meeting her by accident on the street, or perhaps in one of the stores of Tonto's Wickiup. I imagined how sweet and funny and kind and loving she'd be, and then imagined that she'd be simply wretched and not at all the girl I'd guessed when I'd glimpsed her shining face.

That was a little unsettling. I blamed it on Cole, naturally. His actions today had predisposed me to look on the ugly side, the unexpected side.

And I suddenly realized that he hadn't finished whatever it was he had started out to tell me. All he had done was lecture me on the merits of being his puppet, but he'd given me no concrete reasons for playing the part.

Well, tomorrow I'd ask him, straight out, just why he thought that the whole world had seemed to descend upon my head because I had sent a simple wire! It made not a lick of sense to me.

Of course, neither did John Henry Strider, nor Misters Hill or Atbrun. I was totally at a loss.

I tugged off my boots, climbed out of my clothes, and eased into that leviathan of a bed. And despite the muffled giggles and groans coming through the wall, I resisted the temptation to listen by falling directly to sleep.

I rose early the next morning, full of good intentions about writing that long overdue letter to Clive Barrow, and about arranging a meeting with Annie

O'Brien. However, I had barely set pen to paper when there came a knock on my door.

It was Willie. My first thought was that he had come for last night's dirty dishes, but when I moved to get the tray, he said, "There's a feller, Horace. Tate. Boss."

I stopped and turned. "What 'feller?' "

"The one in the street. He's standin' out on the walk, and he keeps hollerin', 'Kid Donovan!' I reckoned that was you. . . ."

"Well, ask him to come in, for heaven's sake," I said, annoyed but curious. "I'll come downstairs in a moment."

But Willie didn't leave. "Already asked him. He said he's callin' you out."

"He's what?"

Willie rolled his eyes. "Callin' you out. Don't you know nothin'?"

"Apparently not," I replied, then tapped my lips. "Is Cole still in the next room?"

"Far's I know."

"All right. Thank you, Willie." I handed him the tray, then marched myself out into the hall and to Belle's door. I had to rap several times, but Belle herself finally straggled to the door and cracked it open an inch.

"Pardon my early intrusion," I said, "but I need to speak with Cole."

"Cole!" she yelled groggily, but at me, not at him. "Horace is here for you!"

I heard a groan in the dark, from behind her.

"I don't know. He didn't say," she replied. It seemed that while his grunts were indecipherable to me, she made them out with no trouble.

He grumbled again.

"What's it about?" she asked. By this time, her eyes were drifting closed again, and I was afraid she'd fall asleep while standing at the doorjamb.

"It's about the gentleman who's calling me out into the street," I said.

This time, I heard a quick rustle of bedclothes, the thud of boots and the jingle of spurs, and the soft curses of a man trying to dress hurriedly. It was as I feared, then. Whoever was out there had come to kill me.

Yet again.

I was growing weary of the gesture.

Belle moved aside, and Cole stepped past her and out into the hall, still buckling his gun belt.

"Who is it?" was all he said.

"I don't know. Willie told me," I replied, then added, "You said I should do nothing without consulting you."

He looked up, and the expression on his face was, well, amused. I didn't quite know how to take it. "That's right, kid. I did. And just what did I stop you from doin' this time?"

"Going out to see what he wanted."

"Good thing you stopped, then." He moved past me and started down the stairs. I followed on his heels. "Probably some quick-draw Johnny lookin' to make his reputation," he said as our boot steps echoed hollow in the empty bar. "Either that, or another one of Johnny Hill's ilk."

He started out across the floor toward the doors, asking, "Willie? You ever seen this yahoo before?"

"New to me, Cole, and about all of twelve years old," Willie replied, polishing a glass.

Cole breathed, "Damn!" under his breath, and pushed through the swinging doors.

I watched him, from inside them. He walked out into the center of the street and shouted, "What you want, son?"

"I want Kid Donovan!" came the answer, and I had to stand to the side to see the young man, braced and ready to draw, a block up the street. He was most certainly not twelve, but he didn't appear to be much older than I.

"What for?" Cole called.

The question appeared to confuse the young man, who hesitated a long moment before he replied, "I wanna kill him! He killed John Henry Strider, didn't he?"

I saw Cole's chest heave with a sigh. His prophecy had come true, after all. He said, "As a matter of fact, son, he didn't. I did. Cole Jeffries is the name. You wanna draw on me?"

The boy's posture changed. He seemed to pull into himself, somehow, and he said, "Huh?"

"I asked if you wanted to call me out, instead,"

Cole said. Once again, I read amusement on his face, although I could see nothing remotely amusing in his situation.

Belle had followed us down the stairs, and she stood at my shoulder, watching the street. I whispered, "What on earth is he doing?"

She put a gentle hand on my arm. "Just playin'," she answered, with a little smile. "Honest. That Cole!"

The boy down the street appeared to be thinking it over, and not too happily. Finally, he said, "D-did you say Cole Jeffries?"

Cole nodded.

"If y'don't mind, sir, I'd a whole lot druther you sent the Kid out."

Cole said, "Well, you're gonna be disappointed, then, ain't you?"

The boy's face screwed up and he looked as if he were about to throw a tantrum when the sheriff moved into view. He leaned against a post across the way, and folded his arms. "Got trouble, Cole?" he asked. Down the street, the boy watched with keen—if nervous—interest.

"Nothin' I can't handle, Walt," Cole said, all confidence and bravado.

"Well, I don't want no fresh bodies in my cemetery today," Sheriff Eli said, and swung his gaze down the way. "You're not from around here. What's your name, boy?"

The lad hesitated, then called, "Joe Turner."

"Well, be off with you, Joe Turner," the sheriff said. "Go on, now. Scat!"

Young Turner threw a glance toward the saloon—and right toward where I was standing, although I don't think he could have seen me in the shadows—then turned and slouched back down the street, toward a horse tied at the rail. He was on his way out of town before Cole relaxed.

"Thanks, Walt," he said with a wave.

"No trouble, Cole," replied the sheriff. "But I'd appreciate if you'd get Heck's boy outta town for a while." He walked off, and Cole came back inside, leaving me to wonder why the sheriff seemed to think it was *my* fault!

Cole walked right past me with no further explanation and muttered, "Beer," at Willie. Then he sat down next to Belle, who waited at Uncle Hector's private table.

"You're alive, darlin'," she said, and kissed his cheek.

"That I am, Belle," he replied, and took her into his arms.

She giggled.

16

If Cole planned on getting me out of town, I was going to make certain he didn't do it before I got to meet Miss Annie O'Brien. While he sat alongside Belle, nursing his beer, I sauntered casually over to the bar and whispered a question to Willie.

"Two blocks south and over one west," he said as he polished a glass. "Can't miss it. It's the white one with the big front porch and the double swings. Why?"

I didn't bother to answer him. I simply thanked him and set off, down the street, letting Cole's "Hey, kid!" ring unheeded, behind me on the air.

I was glad I had taken care when dressing that morning. Uncle Hector's pants and sleeves were a bit long, but a much better fit than my own clothes. And I fancied the blue of the brocade vest looked nice with my eyes. As I neared the O'Brien home, I pushed my hat—one of Uncle Hector's best beaver

Stetsons, actually—down a little lower to disguise my bandaged ear.

The house was as Willie had described it—unmistakable. It was the only wooden house on the block and the largest; it had a long front veranda with a wide porch swing on either side of the front door. I supposed they needed two swings, if they had all those daughters; then I felt heat flood my face when I imagined myself sitting and swinging with Annie. And kissing those bee-stung lips.

I stopped across the street and waited for my face to cool.

I had given much thought to the correct way to approach Annie, and had finally settled on that which I considered most proper. I girded my loins, cleared my throat, and strode across the street, trying to appear full of confidence. I opened the gate of her white picket fence and stepped onto the porch. I knocked.

Almost at the same instant, the door opened, and I believe I jumped a little. There stood Mrs. O'Brien, Annie's mother. I gulped.

"Mornin', son," she said. Her eyes had the same hint of veiled amusement that Cole's had shown earlier, and for a moment I wondered why everyone was laughing at me.

But I collected myself, nodded my head, and said, "Good morning, Mrs. O'Brien. My name is Horace Smith, and I wondered if I might speak to your daughter, Anne."

"You're the new owner of Hanratty's?" she asked, her amused look deepening.

"It seems that word travels quickly in a small town such as this," I said, forcing a smile of my own.

"Yes, it does, Mr. Smith," she replied. She showed no intention of going to fetch Anne, though.

"I hope it's not offensive to you, Mrs. O'Brien. I mean, my having inherited a . . . drinking house. I have every intention of divesting myself of—"

She turned, and called down the hall, "Annie! It's that boy from yesterday!" She turned back to me. And smiled openly. "You can't help the business your uncle was in." She gestured to the porch swing on the right. "Have a seat, Mr. Smith. She'll only be a moment."

"Mr. Smith?" asked the vision before me. I stood, instinctively, although I daresay my knees were knocking.

"C-call me Horace, Miss O'Brien."

Her face screwed up a tad, and she repeated, "Horace?"

"Or you could call me Tate," I quickly added. Perhaps Cole had been correct when he said not to mention my real name to anyone.

"Tate, then. I like that. Won't you please have a seat?"

I did without looking, and was most grateful when my backside met swing instead of porch. She sat beside me, although on the far side of the bench. "And you must call me Annie," she said, folding her delicate hands in her lap. When I sat there, mute and unable to think of a word to offer, she said, "And what brings you here this morning, Tate?"

"I . . . I wanted to meet you, Miss—I mean, Annie," I muttered. "That's all." Actually, I wanted to ask her to be my wife, bear my children, and allow me to spend the rest of my life worshipping her, but that seemed a bit much. At least, for our first meeting. I added, "I wanted to ask your permission to . . . keep company with you."

There. At least I had that part out. And suddenly, I wanted to drop right through the floorboards, lest she say no.

She tipped her head, and the light danced on her corn silk locks and twinkled in her clear blue eyes. "Keep company? But I don't know you, do I? Except that you're polite to ladies on the street, and wave rather than shouting catcalls or whistling."

"What better way is there to get to know each other than to keep company?" I parried.

"True," she said with a nod, and relaxed back into the arm of the swing. "Well, let's get started, shall we? Tell me about yourself, Tate."

I was growing increasingly relaxed with her—and was nearly up to the point where I spent my thirteenth summer in Ontario, with a paid companion—when Pony Girl, of all people, came traipsing up the street. She was dressed in her work clothing, and wore a generous display of face paint. Horrified, I watched as she opened the gate, leaned provocatively on its post, and said, "Hiya, sweetie. Cole wants you back up at the place. Hey, Annie."

I wanted to die.

But Annie smiled and said, "Morning, 'Randa. I was just about to offer Tate a glass of lemonade. Would you care for some?"

While I was still puzzling over the 'Randa part, Pony Girl said, "Thanks, but I gotta get Horace back. Cole's in a toot." Then she frowned at me and said, "C'mon, boss! Daylight's burnin'!"

I rose, although I'll be damned if I remember how. But I do recall asking, as I walked out the gate, "May I call again, Annie?"

And I most assuredly remember her reply, which was "Surely, Tate," delivered with a wondrous smile.

The next thing I knew, I was being pulled back toward Hanratty's by Pony Girl. "Oh, Cole's pitchin' a fit, sugar," she said, attempting to hold her little robe closed with one hand and drag me with the other. "He wants you in there yesterday! What'd you do to piss him off, anyhow?"

"I—I—"

"Stop jawin' and start goin', honey!"

"I am!" I was stumbling over Uncle Hector's boots to keep up with her, as a matter of fact. "Who's 'Randa?"

Pony Girl looked at me as if I had seven eyes and eight ears. "Miranda's me, you fool!" she said, and pushed me through the doors of the bar. "I'm 'Randa!"

"Well, how was I supposed to know?" I asked, even as a hand—connected to Cole—descended upon my shoulder.

"Get movin', kid," he said, and gave me a shove back outside—and down into the dirt. He set out at a brisk clip toward the livery. "Don't worry," he said after I caught up with him. "Belle packed for you." He disentangled my bedroll and saddlebags from his and tossed them to me.

"Why?" I demanded, out of breath and struggling with my gear. "Where are we going?"

"Anywhere but here."

"But—"

"And I thought I told you not to write any letters, goddamn it! Belle found one in your room, half wrote!"

"But it was only to—"

We had reached the livery. Cole stopped and broke in, quite firmly, "When I tell you something, boy, I mean it. No letters. No telegrams. No communicatin' in any way, shape, or form!"

I gulped and blinked. "All right, Cole," I said. "I simply didn't think—"

"That's just the trouble, Donovan," he growled as he grabbed his saddle off the rack. "You don't think."

And I hated him again, because he was right.

*   *   *

We headed south, and were several miles from town before he deigned to speak to me again. "How you feel about Yuma, kid, or maybe Mexico?"

"One is as dismally bleak as the other, I suppose," I said.

Part of me was still back on the O'Briens' porch with Miss Annie, and I couldn't begin to compare the warmth of her back-east-styled home—not a speck of adobe in sight!—with the sorts of shabby dives I imagined Cole would lead me to.

They would probably all be like that place yesterday, made of dried cactus and mud, and reeking of bad whiskey.

"Well, I don't reckon anybody's heard of you in Yuma, yet," he said, more to himself than me. "And they speak English there."

I actually perked up at this tidbit. "Yuma it is," I said, almost eagerly. With all the reasons I had to stay in Tonto's Wickiup—Annie being first on that list—it never crossed my mind to tell Cole I'd rather not go at all. I suppose he had cowed me that much. And also, I suppose that I saw in him something of a father figure, although he was far too young. He certainly acted the part, though.

Cole nodded curtly. "Fine. Yuma."

And then he lapsed back into silence again. After a few minutes had passed, with no sound other than the plod and crunch of Tell's and Ranger's hooves, the swish of brush underfoot, and the gentle creaking of leather, I dared to ask, "Cole? Yesterday, when that Mr. Atbrun tried to . . . I mean, before that, you were telling me something. And you didn't finish. What was it?"

Cole stared at me for a second and I feared I had stirred up a good bit of trouble, but then he said, "Been thinkin' it over, kid. Don't trouble yourself, yet. I'm thinkin' that I need to see a good paper."

"A good paper?"

"A good newspaper. You know, like one from back east, with the whole news in it. Not just the local crud, like back in town."

I said, "Oh." And then, "Why?"

Cole sniffed. "Just gotta check on a couple things, that's all. Don't want to go off half cocked."

I was only more puzzled. I asked, "Do you care to explain that?"

He grinned at me. "Nope," he said, then fanned Ranger's backside and took off at a dead gallop.

I had no choice but to follow.

Three evenings later, after camping out each night and not being snake- or spider-bitten, attacked by wandering camels or bobcats, or swarmed by disgruntled scorpions, we arrived in Yuma. I cannot say the town had much to recommend it, but then, I wasn't expecting much, and it was dark when we rode in.

After sleeping on the hard ground for nights on end, I was looking forward to a hotel bed, even if it did prove a tad buggy.

Cole, however, had other things on his mind.

We didn't even take the time to settle our horses at the livery. At his insistence, we tied them to the rail outside a little place called Cantina de Maria, and went inside, where Cole ordered dinner for both of us, along with a round of cervezas, which he translated for me. Beer.

At least this beer had no flies in it, and I choked down half a warm glass before they brought our supper. This was some foreign concoction that I hadn't understood when Cole ordered it, and still didn't comprehend after he explained it to me.

"That there's your enchiladas, kid," he said, pointing to my plate with his knife. "Beef, or so they say, with lots of goat cheese. Good sauce, too." The knife moved. "Those are *refritos*—that's refried beans to you—and that there's guacamole. Made from avacados. You can spread it on the tortillas," he added, pointing to a curious side dish that looked something like bread, but wasn't.

I stared at him, probably as blank as a sheet of paper just pulled from the notebook.

"Oh, hell," he muttered, disgusted again. "Just eat up." He dug into the mess on his plate.

I watched him for a few seconds. He didn't seem to be seizing up, so I tried a bite of my beans. Surprisingly, they were quite good. I hadn't realized how hungry I was after having shared just one meager jackrabbit with Cole for lunch, and began to eat like a stevedore.

"This is Mexican food?" I said around a mouthful of enchilada. "It's wonderful!"

Cole just nodded and kept on eating. I avoided the little plate of jalapeño peppers that they brought with the meal, however—once burned, twice shy, as they say. Cole ate them all and washed them down with that horrible warm beer, and I kept expecting flames to shoot out of his mouth each time he opened it.

They didn't, though. And for dessert, he ordered us some kind of wonderful custard in caramel sauce, called flan. I must say, I hadn't enjoyed a meal so much in quite some time! Our table was cleared and I was ready to find a hotel, but Cole was not. We sat there, listening to a rather dreadful musical group—which he called a mariachi band—while he downed tequila after tequila and I began to feel rather . . . bloated.

Actually, I was in distress. I tried to ask Cole if there were any outhouses, since he seemed to know the town and the place, but the band was so loud that he couldn't hear me. When I could wait no longer, I stood up to head for the rear door.

I elbowed my way through the crowd standing on the open part of the floor—which, I suppose, was meant for dancing—and was nearly to the far edge of the mob when I heard someone say, "Donovan?"

I turned to find the source of the voice, which was

thickly accented, gruff, and low, and I suddenly realized that the crowd through which I had been working my way was heavily armed, in addition to being rowdy and loud. I couldn't pick out the speaker, though. A cold chill gripped my spine, and I turned toward the rear door once again.

I twisted, only to face a rather broad, muscular Mexican man, thick of mustache and armed to the teeth. He stood there, blocking my way. And he smiled. I cannot say it was the most wholesome smile with which I have been greeted. I backed off a step, fully expecting to bump into some other patron, but there was none there. The floor had cleared, just like that, and I stood alone in the center of the room.

A hush had fallen over the gathering, as well, and for a moment there was no one in the world but myself and that horrid man, who still smiled coldly at me through yellow teeth.

"Donovan!" someone called behind me.

I wheeled once more. Three men stood behind me, spaced an arm's length apart, and any one of them might have called my name. All were staring at me, all were armed, and two were smiling, although none of them appeared particularly friendly. The last of the rest of the mob was quickly funneling out the front door.

I felt the chill in my spine turn to ice.

"*Don-o-van,*" someone said in singsong. And then

it was repeated by a new voice, and another, and another.

A quick glace toward my table told me that Cole had fled me, too. How could he? How could he desert me now?

And then I heard his voice, shouting, "Drop!"

I did! I hit that floor faster than gravity could account for, and landed on my face just as the place exploded with gunfire. It was as if ten cannons went off at once in a confined space, and abruptly my ears were of more concern than my burning bowels.

But I hadn't been shot, I quickly realized and, hands still over my ears, chanced a glance upward.

Another single shot turned my face downward again, and my eyes seemed to seal closed. From that dark, terrifying place, I heard the ring of spurs as boots neared. And then I felt a boot's toe nudge my side. I opened one eye.

"It's all right, kid" came Cole's familiar baritone, which, at that moment, I greeted as the voice of God Himself.

I climbed slowly to my feet, while taking in the six dead men that ringed me. One of them still twitched rhythmically.

"W-what happened?" I asked. I don't imagine it came out very forcefully. "W-was I supposed to ask permission for the outhouse?"

Amazingly, Cole chuckled, which nearly knocked me back to my knees again. However, I managed to hold my ground while he said, "Go on ahead, kid. It's out back."

I took a stiff step before he added, "Just be ready. I'd draw my gun, if I was you."

I complied and slowly made my way to the back door, stepping over two bodies of my would-be murderers along the way.

There was no trouble in the alley, and the outhouse was easy to spot—and to smell. As I sat there in the dark, one hand holding my testicles above seat level, I realized what had happened. Or at least, what I thought must have happened. Those miscreants had surrounded me. If they all fired at once, they would've naturally hit each other, I reasoned. And Cole had been there to take out the one that wasn't felled in the initial blast.

Thank God for Cole!

I decided, right then and there in that dark, dank, wretched outhouse, to cut him in for exactly one half of my profits from the Aztec Princess. As exasperating as he could be, he was my savior many times over and, I realized, the best friend I could possibly have. Even if he did call me by the wrong name.

Needless to say, we didn't stop the night in Yuma. We only stayed long enough for Cole to have some heated words with the sheriff, to most of which I was not privy. We rode a few miles out of town, then camped. By then, I must have imbibed a good half gallon of water—on top of the beer I'd had in town—and had to call a temporary halt to the journey twice. It seemed that Mexican food didn't agree with me, which was a shame, because I very much liked it.

When I explained this to Cole, he just said, "Don't worry, Donovan. You'll get used to it."

I wanted to know just what he meant by that. And I wanted him to offer an explanation of what had gone on while I was facedown on the floor—and later, when he spoke with the sheriff—but Cole was not forthcoming with any information.

This did not surprise me.

I ringed my pallet with my rope, snuggled down into the thin comfort of my blanket, and fell into a fitful slumber.

17

For the next few days, we simply wandered aimlessly. We rode to the edge of a vast and endless sea of drifting white sand, which Cole told me was the Yuma Desert. I have never seen anything so beautiful or so forbidding.

We journeyed across the Colorado River and into California without incident, and I was beginning to relax somewhat. I think Cole was, too. At least, he managed a few words to me.

"John Henry Strider's killin' brought those idiots in Yuma down on you," he said. "Same for that yahoo kid back in Tonto's Wickiup. Well, maybe he wasn't such a yahoo after all. He had the sense to leave, anyway."

"Joe Turner," I reminded him.

"Yeah, whatever. So I figure Yuma and Tonto's Wickiup are Lop Ear and Jingles's fault." He lit the smoke he'd rolled a few minutes before and, as he shook out the match, added, "But Strider himself, and Big John Hill, and Duffer Atbrun, those were different."

"How so?"

"Cause they're hired guns, kid. Their kind don't go round killin' folks unless there's money in it. Or revenge. The first two, I figure for the money part."

"And Atbrun for revenge? Because of Mr. Hill?" I offered. Actually, I was completely lost.

Cole nodded. "Now who in the hell would have call to dislike you so much that they'd hire a killer? It don't seem to me you're old enough to have made any enemies that bad."

I shook my head. "I can't imagine . . ."

"There are more out there you should be worried about. Red Nose Dakota—he's part Crow—Ralph Biggs, Elias Jenkins, and Apache Tom, just off the top o' my head. Guns for hire, every one. Tell me, Donovan. How'd your folks die, anyways?"

I told him the whole story from the beginning, and how Mr. Dean had pressed cash upon me and put me on the train.

He was silent for a few moments before he said, "Well, you've had it hard, Donovan. Mighty hard. Tell me more about this Mr. Dean. I recall old Heck mentionin' him a few times."

I told him everything I knew, which, granted, wasn't much, and then we drifted into silence again.

We decided, however, that perhaps it was safe to go up to the Aztec Princess again to check on the "diggin's," as Cole called them. We turned back east to cross the muddy Colorado again.

Privately, I wondered how long I could actually survive. I had been in the territory less than two weeks, and already had every killer—both amateur and professional—in the West following me around, or so it seemed. As long as Cole was around, I had a good chance, I surmised, but I would have to be alone sometime, wouldn't I?

And there was Annie. My sweet little Annie. Oh, she looked so much more beautiful seen from close up, without a street between us! Those eyes of hers weren't just blue, but sparkling, cornflower blue, and her hair wasn't just blond, it had the color and sheen of corn silk pulled fresh from the field.

And her face! Oh, I could have written sonnets about her face. Except that just then, Cole thumped me in the side.

"Wake up, kid," he said. "We're pullin' in."

The Colorado ferry we had been riding had indeed pulled into its dock across the river, and we led our mounts off. While Cole settled with the ferryman, I stroked Tell's soft neck. He was a beauty, too, and hadn't spooked at the ferry either time we'd ridden it. That is an important thing for a horse, and shows its trusting nature.

I swung a leg up, smoothed his ebony mane into place over those silvery withers, and waited for Cole's return. It was quicker than I'd thought. He fairly leapt to Ranger's back and said, "Ride!"

"Where?" I shouted back, alarmed.

"Just go!" he yelled, and slapped Tell's backside.

Tell almost left me behind, his exit was so hasty! I can't even tell you which direction we took off in, but I can say that it was fast. I clung to the saddle, trying to figure out from whom we were fleeing, while Cole, bent low over Ranger's neck shouted, "This way! Come this way!"

I did.

Soon the terrain changed from gravel and rocks to sand, white sand. I gave Tell his head and prayed that there would be an end, and soon. Both horses were lathered by this time, and Cole showed no indication that he wished to stop, or even slow down.

Over dune after pale, featureless dune we galloped, our horses laboring, sinking deep into the sand, then clattered rapidly over the places where the wind had swept it from the hard substrate. We were climbing yet another of those endless dunes when the first shot came.

It was from behind us, and Cole gestured at me to hurry, hurry. But I couldn't go any faster. Tell was at his limits, and heaved with every breath. I followed Colt to the crest of the dune and was nearly over when, abruptly, another shot sang out, and Tell dropped to his knees.

At first I thought that he had simply given out. In my mind, he was impermeable to bullets. I was the one they were after.

But it was not to be. He lay there, just over the crest,

his breathing labored and a damp red stain blossoming across his belly. I threw myself across his neck, crying, "Tell! Tell, no!" and felt Cole wrench me back by my collar. I tumbled down the dune, white sand sticking to my tear tracks, my heart broken.

"But he's in pain," I shouted at Cole, who had crawled back to his spot, and was peering out, over the top of the hill of sand. "Who did this?" I demanded. "How dare they?"

Cole's head whipped toward me. "Get your ass and your gun up here," he snarled. *"Now!"*

From the top of the dune, the only sounds were the wind's whistle and my poor Tell's labored breaths. I had stopped myself from crying, and tried not to hear them. I looked out across the expanse, and saw nothing.

"Cole . . ." I began.

"Shut up," he said.

I closed my eyes for a moment, wishing for all the world that I had gone over that cliff with Mother and Father, and that none of this had happened, none of it at all. But when I opened my eyes, Tell's sides were still heaving, and the desert was still there.

And a speck of movement.

"There," I said, and pointed. "Something moved at the top of that dune."

"Seen it," said Cole.

"This is my fault again, isn't it?" I was feeling sorry for myself, sorry for Tell, sorry for the world.

"Not this time, kid," he said, his attention on the dunes.

My eyebrows flew up. Not my fault? Not my fault that my horse was dying, not my fault that I was horseless in this desert, not my fault that we were being shot at? I couldn't believe it, couldn't believe Cole.

"Slide down and get my rifle," he said curtly.

Still in a daze, I did as he said. The trip down was much easier than the trip back up, but I made it. And when I at last got back and handed him his rifle, Tell had stopped his labored breathing.

A glance told me he was dead. His sightless eyes stared out over the desert. The air no longer teased his nostrils. Flies had begun to find and settle on his flank injury, and his muscles didn't twitch to shoo them away.

I broke down.

"Knock it off!" came Cole's voice. I didn't look up. All I could think of was my poor Tell, his life stolen by some ne'er-do-well with a grudge.

"I said, knock it off!" This time, Cole hit me in my bad ear, and it started bleeding again, through the bandages. The pain also snapped me to reality, which, I suppose, was what he intended.

"Better," he said, the moment I stopped wailing. "I'm sorry about your horse, kid, but right now, we've got other snakes to—" He cut himself off and fired three rapid rounds at the dune where I had spied movement, then sat there, silently staring, his eyes intent.

My head snapped toward the dune when I heard the scream—thin and distant and very high. Cole waited another moment, then said, "Go get your gear off Tell."

Slowly, I finally moved. I reached Tell's body and, unable to hold my tears back, silently pulled free my saddlebags and pack. He was so beautiful, even in death. I stroked his neck for the last time, then went back to Cole, who was still staring across the sand.

"You got hold of yourself?" he asked without looking up.

My "Yessir" came out in a choked whisper.

"Get down the hill, then."

"But—"

He turned and glared at me.

I slid down the dune's far side once more, and went to where Ranger was standing. When Cole came down, he found me with my arms locked around Ranger's neck and my face buried in his mane.

"It's all right," he said, almost kindly. I heard his rifle slide back into its boot. "Gimme those," he added, and took the gear from my arms. I heard the complaint of leather as he secured my things on his saddle.

And then I felt his hand on my shoulder, which surprised me out of crying further. He said, "It's all right to cry, Horace. I had a first horse, too." And then he swung into the saddle. He held a hand down to me.

"But aren't we going to . . . b-bury him?"

He shook his head. "We have to git. He don't mind, kid. I promise. Now step up."

Grudgingly, I did, but my eyes were on Tell the whole time.

"Who were they?" I asked as we rode away. Ranger was a strong horse, but he could travel no faster than a walk carrying both Cole and me. "Are you sure they're dead? You didn't go check."

"They're the Barlow brothers," he said, keeping his eyes on the trail. We were out of the sand dunes by then, and back in the desert. Brush was beginning to show, low on the ground, although the distance ahead promised more growth. "I saw 'em back there, headed down the river toward us."

"They were in a boat?" I think I asked.

"No, ridin' down alongside the river," Cole said, and I heard him snort. I supposed I deserved it, that time.

"So who are these Barlow brothers?"

"Fellers I knew from . . . from a long time ago. Like I said, sorry, kid."

"You mean that your long-lost past caught up with you?"

I took Cole's silence for assent.

"From when you were down in Mexico?" I added.

He reined in Ranger and said, "Get off."

I did, against my better instincts. I wouldn't have put it past him to just ride off and leave me.

But then he dismounted, too. "Let's let Ranger take a little breather," he said, and began walking and leading the gelding. I kept up with him.

"Why were they trying to kill you?"

Cole looked down at his boots for a moment, then straight ahead again. "Because I killed their daddy."

"And that's why you ran from them? Instead of . . ."

He turned toward me, and he had that amused expression on his face again. He said, "Instead of holdin' my ground and facin' them like a man?"

"I wouldn't have put it exactly that way," I said, trailing off.

"No, I s'pose you wouldn't. But yeah, that's why I took off. Their papa, old Jake—he was one tough customer and meaner than a sack full o' rattlers, but I never had nothin' against those boys of his. They been comin' for me, off and on, for about ten years now. Some people just won't let the past rest."

This time, I was the silent one. I was trying to imagine Cole as a very young man—as El Diablo Dorado—hot-blooded and in a strange land. Was it then that these brothers started coming after him? I wondered. How many more were there? How did he sleep at night, knowing so many people wanted him dead?

"Forgot to ask you," he said, breaking into my

thoughts. "What'd you think of Annie, once you saw her up close?"

"She's beautiful," I replied. Somehow, I didn't want to talk about her so soon after such ugliness. "Were they dead? The Barlow brothers, I mean. How many were there?"

"I don't know, and two. Arlo and Carlo."

I stopped stock-still. "You're joking."

He stopped, too, and his face screwed up. "About what?"

"Arlo and Carlo Barlow?"

His mouth crooked up into a grin and he scratched his head. "Never thought about it that way," he admitted, then laughed. "Well, the third one wasn't so funny. That was Juan. He's not around anymore."

By the way he said it, I thought I'd best not ask what had happened to Juan. I said, "I don't have enough money to buy another horse. Not one as good as Tell, anyway."

We started walking again, and Cole replied, "There won't ever be another one like him for you, Donovan. But we'll try and find you somethin' close."

Later that day, we walked into Yuma and went directly to the livery, where I found a nice chestnut gelding in a horse trader's string. Cole looked him over, but found him lacking. "He's fourteen if he's a day," he said. "Try again."

I picked out a bright buckskin. He had a black

mane and tail, like Tell's, and I suppose I thought
that would be lucky. But Cole said, "Nope. Fistulous
withers. Sorry."

At last, we agreed on a five-year-old gelding,
strawberry roan in color, with the rather feminine
name of Cherry. He wasn't any too pretty, but he
had kind eyes and small, tipped-in, wide-set ears,
and he nuzzled me when I spoke to him. The trader
assured me he was sound and well trained in all
the basics—although he'd not been schooled in any
"ropin' or cuttin' stuff" of which the trader was
aware.

I didn't need a horse trained to cut cattle, although
I said nothing. Cole was doing my negotiating for
me, and for once I had the presence of mind not to
open my mouth. He ended up buying the gelding
for only thirty dollars, and only because "the damn
thing ain't even trained to cut cows!"

Once again, we didn't tarry in Yuma. Cole wanted
to keep moving, and I can't say I had any desire to
argue with him. For all I knew, one or both of the
Barlow brothers were closing in on us, and would
shoot yet another unfortunate horse from beneath
me.

We camped well to the northeast of Yuma, in the
shelter of a little copse of palo verde trees, which are
a most curious creation. They have no leaves and a
sickly green bark, which is, for the most part, smooth.
I found them strange and alien. However, Cherry
was proving a very good horse, although he couldn't

be compared with Tell. His gaits were soft, he was tender of mouth, and even though he had a tendency to be a bit eager, I was most satisfied with him.

This didn't help me from thinking about Tell nearly nonstop, however. I missed him terribly.

Two days later, we came upon the Aztec Princess, and Jingles and Lop Ear greeted us enthusiastically. They had been blasting and the mine had failed to flood, for one thing. And for another, they were finding gold!

"Oh, she's a rich one, all right, young Tate Donovan," Jingles said, cackling. He dug into his pocket and pulled out three chunks of rock, one almost solid gold, and I gasped. "You're goin' to be the richest dang-blasted kid in the territory," he cried. "Mayhap the whole danged country!"

"He'th got him a point," Lop Ear added. He was cooking dinner and Loretta was under his arm, her tail a-wag and her colorful eyes dancing. I wondered how she was hitting it off with the resident bobcat.

"After you strike it rich, young Tate," Jingles went on, "I'd appreciate one of those gold bars like you rich people al'ays have around. Like to add it to my collection!"

"Collection?" I asked, but Cole cut me off.

He said, "You pair o' miscreants got any idea how much it'll take to get this thing up an' runnin'?"

It was a question I had very much wanted to ask, too, and would have thought of it if I hadn't had so much else on my mind.

Jingles rubbed his neck. "Well, I think that's more in Lop Ear's line. I been on my own for a good many years, now." And then he turned his head and shouted into the darkness, "Comanche! Blast you, you rapscallious villain!" He got up directly and disappeared into the murky night, muttering, "I told those boys not to tether their horses so close . . ."

Cole said, "Well?" and stared at Lop Ear.

He simply shrugged and smiled, showing the gap where his two front teeth used to be. Lisping, he said, "Don't figure we need nobody, Cole. Why, Jingles and me been haulin' it out just fine. After we blasted a few feet down that little side spur, we hit the mother lode. Been buryin' our metal bearin' ore down a secret place in case of bandits, so don't you worry none."

He gave a turn to the rabbit frying in his skillet. Loretta licked her chops. "And don't you trouble your mind about floodin'," he went on. "That little trickle that she was is all she's ever goin' to be. Hey, Jingles!" he added, addressing the deep shadows to my far left. "Check Debby for me!"

All sudden impatience, I said, "I wish someone would come to a finite amount. Mr. Dean wishes to know how much to advance me for the costs."

Cole twisted toward me. "He does? And when did this happen?"

His face had gone dark, and suddenly I was afraid to tell him. But I said, "In his t-telegram. The other day."

"I thought he was just askin' after you!"

"He w-was. In a way. He only—"

"Well, I guess I don't need the damn newspaper, do I?" he snapped, and I cringed.

"What's everybody so riled up about?" Jingles called as he entered the campfire's circle of light. "I could hear you all the way over to the horses!"

Cole jabbed a thumb in my direction. "This little fool managed to set the whole of a hired militia on us, that's all."

I blinked. "What?"

"You still got that wire on you?"

"Yes," I said, patting my pockets. "Somewhere . . ."

I produced it at last and handed it to him. Frankly, it went against my most basic beliefs, letting someone else read my mail like that, but at the moment, I was too shocked to do anything else.

He unfolded it unceremoniously, and stared. His teeth clenched and his jaw muscles worked while he read it over and over, and then fairly threw the paper back at me. "You idiot," he snarled. "You blamed fool!"

I scooted away from him, to keep safely out of arm's reach. He was a little too close and a little too angry for my taste. I asked, "What did I do, Cole?"

"That!" he shouted, pointing at the telegram, which had fallen from my hands and was burning to ashes in the fire. And then he jumped to his feet and began pacing. The ensuing spray of dirt barely missed Lop Ear's frying pan.

"I know about this Mr. Dean of yours," he said as he marched back and forth. "Heck was mighty closemouthed, but he told me a lot more than he did most people. I remember him sayin' as how this Dean had sold shares in the Aztec Princess."

"So the gold isn't all mine?" I asked, crestfallen. "How much stock did he sell? I mean, what percentage is left for me?"

Cole waved the question off. He said, "Don't you read? Don't you know nothin'?"

He stopped and threw his arms wide. "Y'know, it struck me funny at the time, why anybody'd want to buy shares in a dried-up ol' silver mine. But I figured Heck knew best. It was his mine, after all." He dropped his arms and resumed pacing—head down, arms folded. "I think Heck managed to get himself—and your folks, too—killed. And all because of this goddamned hole in the ground!"

Lop Ear looked up, cocked his good eyebrow, and said, "Damn hole in the ground? Well, now, Cole, she's a lot better than—"

Jingles, now returned and standing across the fire, hissed, "Shut up, you ol' rake face."

Lop Ear started to respond, but after one look at Jingles, he closed his mouth.

Cole simply stalked off, into the night. I heard him out there, kicking rocks and muttering.

"Rabbit's done!" Lop Ear cried joyfully.

18

Cole recounted his suspicions the next day, while we were riding aimlessly north. He thought that Mr. Dean was most probably a stock swindler. Now this was a very strong charge, but I'll admit he had the circumstantial evidence to back it up.

He told me that Misters Dean and Cummings had suggested taking the mine public three years after it had completely stopped producing. That struck me as odd—I mean, in that Uncle Hector had agreed to it at all—but Cole said Uncle Hector had told him it was a common practice, and he'd need the money to put new machinery in the Lucky Seven.

Cole said he hadn't thought any more about it, until I mentioned having sent the telegram scant days before John Henry Strider faced off with me at Janeway's, only to be shot and killed. Strider was famous nationwide, Cole said, as a hired gun for the mine interests. It wouldn't have been at all difficult for Mr. Dean to locate and wire him, and send him after me.

But still, I was stuck on the first question I had asked—why?

"Let's backtrack, kid," Cole said. "Your uncle Heck sent his wire, askin' for a stake, about a month or six weeks before your folks died, right?"

"Yes," I replied carefully. "They were just leaving for the Continent when his telegram arrived."

"And they got killed about three days after their ship docked, right?"

"Yes. But—"

"And your uncle Heck, he was killed about a month or so after they were," he broke in. "Then somebody took a shot at me."

"And killed your horse." My mind was on dead horses at the moment. "They killed your Brownie."

"Well," Cole went on, "it seems to me like a lot of people get killed after sendin' off a telegram to Mr. Dean about that mine."

"But Father didn't send . . ." I began, then added, "Oh." He had shown it to Misters Dean and Cummings. He had always shared what he called Uncle Hector's "begging wires" with Aloysius Dean.

Cole had been right last night. I was an idiot.

"Misters Dean and Cummings have oversold the mine, haven't they?" I asked dully, feeling as if I had just been punched in the stomach.

"Bingo!" Cole said and rolled himself a smoke.

I also knew that if another strike of any kind were

made in the Aztec Princess, it would ruin Dean and Cummings. I had read about such things—selling many more shares than there actually were in a property—and although I had no idea just how much of the Aztec Princess had been sold, I knew that it was likely more than she was worth, or could ever produce. I suddenly felt violently sick to my stomach, and leaned over Cherry's side—and my knee—to vomit on the desert floor.

"You got that right, kid," Cole commented, while he lit his cigarette and I scrubbed at my lips with my neck scarf.

The more I thought about this business, the worse it got. By the time we had eaten lunch and moved on again, my mind had embroiled Misters Dean and Cummings in the most malevolent of schemes, in which my entire family were merely pawns.

I had also decided they had more than likely stolen Father's money, and that he had been innocent all along.

I will admit it did not take much self-convincing for me to believe my father blameless. Father may have had his humbugs—Irish maids among them—but a born thief, he was not. Not Theodore Smith!

When we made camp for the night, I asked Cole how many shares he thought Dean and Cummings might have sold.

"You got me," he replied. He loosened his girth and pulled the saddle from Ranger's back. "Maybe six, seven times what there really was to sell."

My jaw dropped. "Six or seven times?"

He shrugged, and put the saddle down. "Happens," he said. "I knew a fella once, sold one hundred percent of his mine shares nine times over."

At long last, we sat down on our blankets and Cole fixed a supper of biscuits and beans. At least we were in no immediate danger. The Barlow brothers seemed to have vanished from our trail, and no one knew where we were, even me.

And if Cole knew, he wasn't telling.

A few days of travel later, we were both sick of campfire cooking and sleeping beneath the stars. We had gone quite a distance north, and Cole said we were near the town of Diablo.

This name gave me some qualms, I will admit. I had seen more men die in the last few weeks than anyone should expect to observe, and wasn't looking forward to another fiasco such as we had experienced in Yuma.

"It's a pretty damned rough place," said Cole, when I voiced my reservations. "But we have to pick us up some chuck. I don't believe I can squeeze another feed out of the beans, and we're gettin' short on grain for the horses, too."

"Very well, then," I said, resigned to the situation. "We can't hide forever."

Actually, what I was thinking was that I had been victimized—not by God, or the Fates, or whatever one wished to call it, but by a man: Mr. Aloysius

Dean. I couldn't fight God, but I could bloody well fight a person! I could fight for my father's good name, and mine.

Let their minions come, I decided. Misters Dean and Cummings would not win.

We rode into Diablo a little before dusk. It was a ramshackle place. Poorly built buildings rose from the ground like ill-spaced teeth, and on either side were canyon walls. One rode down into Diablo, rather than found it on the flat, and the main road ran the length of the canyon.

Most of the people I saw—of which there were few—appeared disreputable and dangerous, not to put too fine a point on it. There was not a female in sight.

It crossed my mind that the future husband of Miss Annie O'Brien should not be caught dead in such a place. And then I shuddered when I realized it was possible I would be.

Eyes followed us as we rode down that dusty excuse for a street. Heads turned slightly with our passage, as if no one wished to officially recognize us, but all knew who we were. I had a very bad feeling again, and was happy I had nothing left in my stomach to throw up.

While I fought the uneasiness in the pit of my belly, we stopped before a livery and arranged for our horses. Then I followed Cole across the street, to what passed as a mercantile.

While he ordered beans and flour and canned

peaches and ammunition, I stared out through the windows, at the street. The few men we had passed on our way into town were gathering now, in little knots along the street, and an ominous sense of foreboding filled me.

"Hey, kid!" Cole called from the counter, breaking into my thoughts. I turned to face him. He said, "Grab a couple of those blankets from the shelf there. No tellin' how long we'll be out here, and the nights are gettin' bone cold now that we're up in altitude."

I went to the back of the store and pulled down two new blankets, both brown and nondescript, and took them to the counter, where I placed them on the mounting pile of Cole's purchases.

"Thanks," he muttered. He rummaged in his purse and paid the storekeeper, asking if we could leave the items and pick them up later. The storekeeper nodded in the affirmative, and Cole said, "Let's go see about grain, and then . . . I'm thirsty, kid. How about you?"

I shrugged. I supposed that it didn't much matter one way or the other. When Cole was thirsty, we drank.

Rather, he drank and I gagged.

He led me up the street to the feed and grain, and then next door, to the saloon. This turned out to be a very poor excuse for a bar, in which we found three rickety tables with two scarred chairs apiece, and a bartop consisting of a raw plank balanced on two barrels. It was little better than those makeshift "places of business" in Tombstone, which I was beginning to think of as the Prince of Cities.

Cole pushed a squawking hen from the closest table and indicated that I should sit down, then crossed the room and leaned over the plank. "Two beers," he said to the bartender, who made our rough and muscular Willie, at Hanratty's, look like a scholar and a gentleman. He had exactly four teeth that I could see—one upper front tooth, an eyetooth, and two lower incisors—and they were all four mossy and gray-green.

Cole didn't seem to think this odd, though, and joined me without comment. Our beers arrived—unfortunately—and while I played with my mug and Cole drank, I let my thoughts drift to happier things. Miss Annie, for instance.

How I wished that I was safe in Tonto's Wickiup and ensconced on her lovely porch swing, and that she was there beside me, laughing at my stories, batting those big blue eyes, and asking me if I wanted lemonade.

What a life I would have, if only I lived long enough to see it! I pined for her.

That was, until Cole tugged my sleeve to get my attention, and then nodded toward the window. Outside, on the walk, one of those little knots of men had moved close and swelled in number. Six or eight men conversed among themselves, but glanced up and in through the window on occasion, then turned quickly back to the group.

We were being sized up, I thought.

Apparently, Cole thought so, too, and quickly grabbed my untouched beer. "Hate to waste it," he said in a mumble, and tipped the glass to his lips, all the time keeping his attention on the street.

He put the mug back on the table, and said, "C'mon."

I did. I followed him out the back door and into an alley, of sorts, then to the edge of the building.

"Who is it?" I whispered.

He checked his gun. "Red Nose Dakota, Elias Jenkins, and the Hastings boys," he said, keeping his voice low. "Among others."

"And who are they after?" I pressed him. "Me or you?"

"Good question," he replied. "But it's probably you. You go that way," he said, pointing back to the other side of the saloon. "I'm goin' out here." He slipped away, against the side of the building. I followed his instructions and went the opposite way.

Pistol in hand, I crept forward along the opposite side of the building, nervous sweat coursing from my brow and dripping from the end of my nose. I hoped the men in the street had come for me, I admit. It may sound crass, but if I was to die today, I didn't want it to be for something Cole had done in Mexico, while I was still in diapers!

Just then, Red Nose—or so I guessed from the strawberry birthmark that covered his olfactory prominence—turned round the corner and faced me.

He appeared as surprised as I and immediately raised his gun. But mine was already raised, and I fired.

I hit him in the shoulder, and the shot spun him around and back. He didn't go all the way down, though, and fired, crying, "Horace Smith, you little shit!"

I felt the bullet sting my forearm, but I still fired again. This time, he fell straight backward, the slug having hit him in the throat. I saw the blood bubble, then stop, and I immediately retraced my steps.

I was nearly back to the alley again and feeling the bitter sensation of bile collecting in my throat, when two more shots split the silence. "Cole!" I shouted, and ran to the street again.

I rounded the corner just in time to see one man dead in the street—besides Red Nose, that was—and Cole diving down behind the horse trough across the road. He didn't appear to be hurt, though, and I immediately fired on the man who appeared to be shooting at him, and who had just that moment glanced over at me. He was a mere ten feet away and hadn't heard me come around the corner, so it wasn't really fair. Still, I admit that I shot him dead without a second thought.

More shots. I dodged behind the building's corner and watched Cole's head come up as he fired down the street, then ducked again.

"Where?" I shouted.

"This side of the livery!" came his cry.

I didn't think. I only reacted. I sped off, holding my arm and running alongside the saloon and back to the alley, then down it until I reached the last building before the livery. The hostler had turned all the horses out before fleeing the hail of bullets, and they stood between my position and the gunman's. Between Ranger's legs, I could plainly see him—or at least bits of him—crouched in the open side door of the stable, firing at Cole.

I did the only thing I could think of. I lay down on my belly and tried to find a clear shot between the horse's legs. But every time Ranger moved out of the way, Cherry or another innocent horse took his place.

At last, I gave up and moved forward, I suppose with some idea of skirting the rear of the corral and getting behind the gunman. I had almost accomplished it and was nearly to my goal when the gunman abruptly twisted toward me and opened fire. It was nearly in one motion, so I had no time to dive out of the way, although I tried, too late.

His slug bit deep into my thigh, and the wound sprayed blood through the air as I landed behind the stable, tears stinging my eyes. The blood was flowing freely, but at least I had the presence of mind to pull the bandanna from my neck and tie a hasty tourniquet.

I pulled myself to my feet once more. Stumbling one-legged to the back door of the barn, I finally paused at its edge and peeked around the door. The gunman, having apparently given me up for dead, was firing up the street again.

I managed to creep inside, and actually aimed my gun at his back.

I had a clear shot.

I could have fired.

Something held me back, though. At least, until another man slid into the stable's front doors and took a shot at me. He hit me in the leg—again, although this time in my calf—and when I fired, he went over backward. My second shot was for the alerted first gunman, though, who was wheeling to take aim even as I pulled the trigger. And in doing this in such rapid succession, I lost my balance and fell to the floor, knocking over a bucket of water on my way down.

His shot went wild and he hit nothing but the rafters. But my returned fire pushed him backward in the mucky straw and out into the corral amid the milling horses' hooves. I shot him in the chest.

I toppled to the ground, holding my hurt leg, the blood thick and sticky on my fingers and palm. I remember thinking that a man wasn't supposed to lose this much blood and live. When I looked up, I realized that I had disturbed more than a bucket.

In the stall behind me, a broken lantern had set fire to the straw on the floor. Flames were already climbing the wall. I tried to get to my feet, failed, and ended up crawling out the front door, past the dead man who lay there, and dragging a bucket. I suppose I had some foolish idea that I'd get to the water and put the fire out.

I was halfway between the doors and the blacksmith's water trough, just outside, when I heard a burst of fresh shots, and did my best to hurriedly crawl back inside the burning building.

I couldn't see the men involved. I couldn't even see Cole. He'd moved from behind the trough up the street to God knows where.

Men were up there somewhere, though, freely exchanging shots across the wide-open street.

But I realized they hadn't seen me yet.

Smoke roiled wildly in the freshening breeze of evening. Flames devoured old straw, fueled by dry manure and the detritus of years. I heard a window explode.

It was at this point that I realized I couldn't save the livery. I crawled in to rescue the only creature still trapped inside, a rabbit locked in its hutch, and set it free. On both hands and a knee, dragging one leg behind me, I followed it out the front doors, albeit somewhat more slowly.

By the time I had crawled halfway across the street, keeping my head low and pulling my leg as stiffly as possible, the whole place was engulfed. One of the horses broke down the corral's gate, and Cherry and Ranger raced off into the distance—after narrowly missing me—along with three or four other mounts.

I looked up the street again, toward the gunfire.

In the fading light, the small traces of gunshots—powder flares—were vaguely visible on the side of the street I had come from. I wondered if I should cross back over the street and attempt to sneak up from behind them, or whether I would do better to continue on my original path.

I admit that I also tested my leg, seeing if I could move it—I could, although with immense pain—and making certain that neither bullet had hit bone. I had forgotten completely about my arm.

In the end, I followed my original course, and made it the rest of the way across the street, opposite the fiery livery.

Intermittent shots continued to slice the evening stillness. The livery, cobbled together from what I was sure were very old, dry boards, was blazing away, and sparks had caught the buildings on either side afire. I feared the whole town would go that way, as no one, including the stableman, had come running to fight it. It seemed everyone in town was either in the gunfight or hiding from it.

I tried to crawl up the street, but I was growing weaker by the moment. Additionally, I was losing a great deal of blood—my tourniquet had little effect, no matter how tightly I twisted it—and a terrible cold seemed to grip my bones. I made it a few feet before I could go no further.

Consciousness began to slip from me, and the last thing I thought to do—the *only* thing I could think to do—was to fire my gun several times and draw their fire down the street. I remember thinking that I did not have much time left, and that it didn't really matter if I were shot again.

I emptied my gun straight up middle of the road. The gun slipped from my fingers.

I saw no more.

I was shocked to open my eyes and see daylight, and not the daylight surrounding Diablo, either. We were back down at the Aztec Princess—although how we'd gotten there I had no idea—and Jingles was bending over me. His mouth popped open in surprise and he yelled, "Hot diggity and pass the biscuits! He's awake! And alive!"

Then he clasped me by the shoulders and kissed me with a loud smack, right in the middle of my forehead. "You're alive, young Donovan! Alive and breathin'!"

I hardly knew what to do. And I had no time to do it in, for Lop Ear, Cole, and Loretta all crowded in right then, and an enthusiastic Loretta began to lick me from collar to hairline.

"Well," said Cole with a grin. He pushed his hat back. "I'll be damned. Thought you were a goner for sure. Welcome back, boy!"

I was in a weakened state, but I attempted bravado. "You didn't think I'd die and leave this mine in your laps, now, did you?" I asked, and tried to lever myself up. I failed miserably, and fell back upon the blankets, weak as the proverbial kitten.

Jingles chuckled and Lop Ear lisped, "There you go, boy! Want me to hit you up alongthide the head while you're at it?"

I looked toward Cole. "What happened? What day is it?"

"You've been out for three days, Donovan," he said. "I was pretty damn sure we were goin' to lose you for a while there."

"But how'd we get here?"

"After those last eight or nine got through shootin' at me—and by the way, thanks for that last salvo you made—I wandered down and found you. Right careless of you, kid, losing that much blood. Don't do that again."

I smiled, I think. "I'll try not to." And then I belatedly added, "There were eight or *nine* of them up there?"

Cole settled back on his heels, and Jingles and Lop Ear walked to the mine's entrance, arguing—once more—over the Lost Tribe of Israel. Cole nodded as if his entire life had been nine-to-one and the matter was worthy of no exposition, and said, "I walked down the street and whistled up Ranger, and he brought Cherry and a couple others in with him. After I cauterized your leg and arm, I packed you down here."

I remember the cauterizing of my ear, and was most thankful I had been unconscious for this occasion. I gulped. "Over Cherry's back?"

"Just like a sack of feed," he said with a smile. "I

pulled us some new saddles off the horses on the rail,'' he added. ''You're riding Red Nose Dakota's rig, I think. I've got Elias Jenkins's.''

When I began to protest, he cut me off, saying, ''Ours were in the livery. What started that fire, anyway?''

''Me,'' I admitted.

''Well, you done a damn good job of it. Took out near the whole town before it burned itself out.''

I closed my eyes, wishing that it would all go away. Now I was doomed to be jailed for arson, if I wasn't first killed by some fool with a gun and a grudge.

But Cole, seeming to read my mind, said, ''I wouldn't worry about anybody comin' after you for that. The whole damn town was put together with spit instead of nails. Blows down or falls down every few years, anyhow. I don't reckon a good fire could be much tougher to repair.''

I heaved an internal sigh of relief, opened my eyes, and said, ''Thank you, Cole. For saving me yet again, I mean.''

He sat back, grunting. ''You know, ol' Red Nose Dakota had a grudge against me from a long time ago. Least I could do for the feller who killed him, now, wasn't it?'' And he smiled at me.

I grinned back.

Postscript

Dear Trey,

Well, as I said, it's been years since those events, and the world has changed a great deal in that time. No longer is this a country where men make their own laws and freely murder one another, just to see who's the fastest hand with a gun. Except in Chicago, where, until recently, gangsters shot one another over pin money and liquor.

I never did ascertain just how Cole managed his escape from those villains that day in Diablo. He was never one to talk at any length, and frankly, I wasn't in the mood to press him. I was in the process of learning to just let some things be, or, as Cole would say, learning not to prod every beehive I came across with a short stick. Most bees, I had discovered, did just fine on their own.

But we had survived, and that was the important

part. It is even more important to note that our gun battle in Diablo put a quick end to most of the unpleasantness.

Upon our return to Tonto's Wickiup, Cole sent telegrams to the territorial governor as well as to some old friends in New York—although how he managed to have friends so far away, I can't imagine—and the next thing we heard, Misters Dean and Cummings had been arrested. Both of them served a long time in jail, too, and the scandal was horrendous.

You perhaps recall reading about the Great Stock Swindle of 1882 when you were at Yale, wherein a couple of thimble-rigging brokers had sold up to twelve thousand percent of a number of worthless Western mines? I was at the heart of uncovering it, my boy. Cole and I both.

Cole helped me get things straightened out on my end, and I retained a new attorney, back east, to see to the final details.

In the end, we waited a good year before bringing in any of the gold from the Aztec Princess. Cole said it would just complicate things if we announced a strike while all the paperwork was being sorted out. As it was, we never really announced a strike at all. Jingles and Lop Ear, who were having the time of their lives between the gold and the blasting, rigged up a shack where the old miner's quarters had been, got the pump working again, and even hitched Debby and Comanche to an *arrastra*, to grind the ore.

They smelted it fresh from the ground—although I still have no idea how they ever constructed a kiln hot enough to do it—poured and stamped their own bars, and sold them in California. That is, with the exception of one rough bar, which Jingles carried beneath his wagon seat until his death.

To this day—well, up until 1933, anyway, and the Gold Recall Act—I wondered where the gold in my coins and your grandmother's jewelry came from, and if it was mined at the Aztec Princess. I suppose that most of it now resides at Fort Knox, guarded behind steel doors. A shame. Whenever I touched a gold coin, I felt that a little of me, and Clay, and Jingles and Lop Ear, as well as all the girls was back there, in Tonto's Wickiup: young and carefree and alive.

The mind can play tricks, can't it?

But I was telling you what happened afterward.

I married Annie, of course. We spent the rest of that year swinging on her front porch and sipping lemonade and laughing together and getting to know each other, and were wed on the following Christmas Day. We were very young, of course, but it was the fashion in the West to marry young and we truly loved each other. Still do. Your grandmother is my world.

Hanratty's was a little more difficult to deal with, and I stayed in the whoring game for another few years, albeit only publicly. I had to have a place of business in order to explain the income from the

Aztec Princess, you see. Belle ran the place, although I went to the saloon each afternoon and came home again each night. I unofficially gave Hanratty's to her on my wedding day, and officially turned it over three years later, on Christmas, by which time I had reached my full and preposterous height of six feet, five inches, and added another fifty-five pounds to my skeletal frame.

By that time, Annie—who never measured in at more than five feet, two inches—and I had quite a substantial nest egg saved up and had built the biggest house in town. We also had your dear father. And by then, no one would have mistaken the prosperous family man Mr. Smith for gangly Kid Donovan.

The legends grew, though. Kid Donovan was credited—or damned—with more kills than smallpox, and was rumored to be in Mexico, waiting for the heat to die down. We simply let him stay there.

Cole stayed around town, more or less. And on more than one occasion, he saved my life by stepping from the shadows at just the right moment, guns blazing. For the most part, though, the threat to my life had gone away, simply vanished in the billowing smoke of Diablo. I suppose that leaving that many dead and an entire town in ruin tends to put off the weaker sisters.

Cole married Belle at long last, some seven years after Annie and I wed. Annie and I held their wedding in our home, in the parlor. Jingles and Lop Ear came up for it, along with Loretta and the rest of the creatures. We had to ground-tie Comanche out in the vacant lot next door, for by that time he had tried to savage Debby, Lop Ear's mule, and even I had to admit that the silly old swayback posed a threat.

Lop Ear passed from this earthly plane in 1905. He died in his sleep, long after he and Jingles had cleaned out the Aztec Princess, and went to his rest a happy man. I was awfully glad for that. Annie and I took in Loretta's replacement, a bubbly, shaggy herding dog of the same type—what they're calling, these days, an Australian Shepherd—and she had four more years with us. She was your father's dog and his constant companion.

Jingles died somewhere down around Tombstone at the turn of the century, and not of old age. He was blasting in his new mine, and didn't make it outside before the charge went off. Cole went down to see about him. He said it appeared Jingles had suffered a heart attack during his escape run, and never knew what had hit him.

Cole buried him with his gold bar from the Aztec Princess, and one more that he carried alongside it for all those years. Jingles never did divulge where that one came from, so I think it was likely better off entombed with him.

When your father was fifteen, your grandmother and I moved to Phoenix. There wasn't much left of Tonto's Wickiup by that time, and I was in the state legislature by then. We thought Phoenix made more sense. We bought the big green house that you remember from your childhood, when you came to visit us with your mother.

Your father went off to Yale, and we waited patiently for statehood. It came in 1912, the year your uncle Cole left to follow in your father's footsteps at college. We, in Arizona, were the last state to join the Union, and justifiably so. We were the wildest of the wild places.

Cole left his gunfighting, ruffian ways behind, and he and Belle tried ostrich farming outside of Phoenix. Sometimes he would compete in a local rodeo, or one of the quick-draw contests. He usually won when riding broncs, and always did when the contest was any with a gun.

When ostrich plumes went out of fashion, he went into turquoise mining. He and Belle had three fine children, who grew up to become pillars of Phoenix society, and a testament to good stock coming from bad beginnings.

He tried to enlist when the Great War came, but they turned him down. Too old. If they had taken him, I daresay the war would have been over in a week.

Belle passed peacefully in 1920, and just two years later, Cole was out working in the garden when he was shot dead. We never learned who did it, although their youngest daughter, Rose, was home. She said she ran outside at the sound of the blast, only to see the dust of a rider galloping away.

I never said as much to Rose, but I like to believe

it was a surviving Barlow brother who had done the evil deed. Then, at least, Cole's own past would have sealed his fate.

I could make better sense of it that way, I suppose.

I was known as Tate Smith from the time we rode back into Tonto's Wickiup, and thereafter. It seemed easier to handle than all the trouble that both "Horace" and "Donovan" had brought me. And we carried it on. Your father was Horace Tate Pemberton Smith Jr., but we called him H.T. And you were the third Horace, called Trey.

There seemed to be some degree of symmetry in this.

So you see, there is more myth than truth in the story of Kid Donovan. I never did most of the things that they said I did. Some of "my" efforts were never done by anyone, and a few of the rest by someone else, mainly Cole. I supposed that the press was hungry for someone new to deify or laud and the carnage at Diablo—and that which led up to it—gave them their wish—that was all. It was an accident of time and place, and a case of the fourth estate taking unfair advantage.

I don't know how many died that day in Diablo. I myself can only account for three—and the fire—and I have asked my Lord and Savior for forgiveness. Cole's body count, on the other hand, will forever remain a mystery. As will most everything about him.

I never had a better friend than Cole Jeffries, and I very much doubt anyone else has, either.

Oh, and I never did write to Clive Barrow, although a year later, I anonymously sent him a snakeskin hatband along with a hat to go under it. The whole affair was just too complicated to explain.

You understand, don't you?

I hope that Clive did.

Love,
Grandfather

The Pre-Civil War Series by
Jason Manning

WAR LOVERS
0-451-21173-1

Retired war hero Colonel Timothy Barlow returns as
right-hand man to President Jackson when there's
trouble brewing on the border—trouble called the
Mexican-American War.

APACHE STORM
0-451-21374-2

With Southern secession from the Union in the East,
the doomed Apaches in the West are determined to die
fighting. But Lt. Joshua Barlow is willing to defy the
entire U.S. Army to fight the Apaches on his own terms.